THE MAN WHO LOST HIMSELF

Published @ 2017 Trieste Publishing Pty Ltd

ISBN 9780649382248

The man who lost himself by H. de Vere Stacpoole

Edited by Trieste Publishing Pty Ltd.
Cover @ 2017

www.triestepublishing.com

H. DE VERE STACPOOLE

THE MAN WHO LOST HIMSELF

 Trieste

The Man Who Lost Himself :: By H. de Vere Stacpoole,

Author of "The Pearl Fishers," "In Blue Waters," "The Reef of Stars," The Starlit Garden," etc. :: :: :: :: :: ::

LONDON: HUTCHINSON & CO.
PATERNOSTER ROW :: :: 1918

CONTENTS

PART I

PART II.

PART III.

CONTENTS

THE MAN WHO LOST HIMSELF

PART I

CHAPTER I

JONES

IT was the first of June, and Victor Jones, of Philadelphia, was seated in the lounge of the Savoy Hotel, London, defeated in his first really great battle with the thing we call life.

Though of Philadelphia, Jones was not an American, nor had he anything of the American accent. Australian born, he had begun life in a bank at Melbourne, gone to India for a trading house, started for himself, failed, and become a rolling stone. Philadelphia was his last halt.

With no financial foundation, Victor and a Philadelphia gentleman had competed for a contract to supply the British Government with Harveyized steel struts, bolts and girders ; he had come over to London to press the business, he had interviewed men in brass hats, slow-moving men who had turned him over to slower-moving men. The Stringer Company, for so he dubbed himself, and Aaron Stringer, who had financed him for the journey, had wasted three weeks on the business, and this morning their

5

tender had been rejected. Hardmans, the Pittsburg people, had got the order.

It was a nasty blow. If he and Stringer could have secured the contract, they could have carried it through all right. Stringer would have put the thing in the hands of Laurenson, of Philadelphia, and their commission would have been enormous. A stroke of the British Government's pen would have filled their pockets; failing that, they were bankrupt. At least Jones was.

And justifiably you will say, considering that the whole business was a gigantic piece of bluff. Well, maybe; yet on behalf of this bluffer I would put it forward that he had risked everything on one deal, and that this was no little failure of his, but a disaster naked and complete.

He had less than ten pounds in his pocket, and he owed money at the "Savoy." You see, he had reckoned on doing all his business in a week, and if it failed—an idea which he scarcely entertained—on getting back third-class to the States. He had not reckoned on the terrible expenses of London, or the three weeks' delay.

Yesterday he had sent a cable to Stringer for funds and had got as a reply : "Am waiting news of contract."

Stringer was that sort of man.

He was thinking about Stringer now as he sat watching the guests of the "Savoy," Americans and English, well-to-do people with no money worries, so he fancied. He was thinking about Stringer and his own position, with less than ten pounds in his pocket, an hotel bill unreceipted, and three thousand miles of deep water between himself and Philadelphia.

Jones was twenty-four years of age. He looked thirty. A serious-faced, cadaverous individual, whom, given three guesses, you would have judged to be a Scotch free kirk minister in mufti, an actor in the melodramatic line, a food crank. These being the three most serious occupations in the world.

In reality he had started life, as before said, in a bank, educated himself in mathematics and higher commercial methods by correspondence, and, aiming to be a millionaire, had left the bank and struck out for himself in the great tumbling ocean of business.

He had glimpsed the truth. Seen the fact that the art of life is not so much to work oneself as to make other people work for one, to convert, by one's own mental energy, the bodily energy of others into products or actions.

Had this Government contract come off, he would have, and to his own profit, set a thousand hammers swinging, a dozen steel mills rolling, twenty ships lading; hammers, mills and ships he had never seen, never would see.

That is the magic of business, and when you behold roaring towns and humming wharves, when you read of raging battles, you see and read of the work of a comparatively small number of men, gentlemen who wear frock coats, who have never handled a bale, or carried a gun, or steered a ship with their own hands. Magicians!

He ordered a whisky-and-soda from a passing attendant, to help him think some more about Stringer and his own awful position, and was taking the glass from the salver when a very well-dressed man, of his own age and build, who had entered by the passage leading up from the American bar, drew his attention.

This man's face seemed quite familiar to him, so much so that he started in his chair as though about to rise and greet him. The stranger, also, seemed for a second under the same obsession, but only for a second ; he made half a pause and then passed on, becoming lost to sight beyond the palm trees at the entrance. Jones leaned back in his chair.

His memory, vaguely and vainly searching for the name to go with that face, was at fault. He finished his whisky-and-soda and rose, and then strolled off, not heeding much in what direction, till he reached the book and newspaper stand, where he paused to inspect the wares, turning over the pages of the latest best seller without imbibing a word of the text.

Then he found himself downstairs in the American bar, with a champagne cocktail before him.

Jones was an abstemious man, as a rule, but he had a highly strung nervous system, and it had been worked up. The unaccustomed whisky-and-soda had taken him in its charge, comforting him and conducting his steps, and now the bar-keeper, a cheery person, combined with the champagne cocktail, the cheeriest of drinks, so raised his spirits and warmed his optimism that, having finished his glass, he pushed it across the counter and said, " Give me another."

At this moment a gentleman who had just entered the bar came up to the counter, placed half a crown upon it, and was served by the assistant bar-keeper with a glass of sherry.

Jones, turning, found himself face to face with the stranger whom he had seen in the lounge, the stranger whose face he knew, but whose name he could not remember in the least.

Jones was a direct person, used to travel and the forming of chance acquaintanceships. He did not hang back.

" 'Scuse me," said he. " I saw you in the lounge, and I'm sure I've met you somewhere or another, but I can't place you ! "

CHAPTER II

THE STRANGER

THE stranger, taking his change from the assistant bar-tender, laughed.

" Yes," said he, " you have seen me before ; often, I should think. Do you mean to say you don't know where ? "

" Nope," said Jones ; he had acquired a few American idioms. " I'm clear out of my reckoning. Are you an American ? "

" No ; I'm English," replied the other. " This is very curious ; you don't recognize me—well, well, well, let's sit down and have a talk, maybe recollection will come to you—give it time—it is easier to think sitting down than standing up."

Now, as Jones turned to take his seat at the table indicated by the stranger, he noticed that the bar-keeper and his assistant were looking at him as though he had suddenly become an object of more than ordinary interest.

The subtlety of human facial expression stands un-challenged, and the faces of these persons conveyed the impression to Jones that the interest he had suddenly evoked in their minds had in it a link with the humorous.

When he looked again, however, having taken his

9

seat, they were both washing glasses with the solemnity of undertakers.

" I thought those guys were laughing at me," said Jones. " Seems I was wrong, and all the better for them. Well, now, let's get to the bottom of this tangle—who are you, anyway ? "

" Just a friend," replied the other. " I'll tell you my name presently, only I want you to think it out for yourself. Talk about yourself, and then, maybe, you'll arrive at it. Who are you ? "

" Me," cried Jones. " I'm Victor Jones, of Philadelphia. I'm the partner of a skunk by name of Stringer. I'm the victim of a British Government that doesn't know the difference between tin-plate and Harveyized steel. I'm a man on the rocks."

The flood-gates of his wrath were opened, and everything came out, including the fact of his own desperate position.

When he had finished, the only remark of the stranger was :

" Have another ? "

" Not on your life," cried Jones. " I ought to be making tracks for the consul or somewhere to get my passage back to the States—well, I don't know. No ; no more cocktails. I'll have a sherry, same as you."

The sherry having been dispatched, the stranger rose, refusing a return drink just at that moment.

" Come into the lounge with me," said he. " I want to tell you something I can't tell you here."

They passed up the stairs, the stranger leading the way, Jones following, slightly confused in his mind but full of warmth at his heart, and with a buoyancy of spirit beyond experience. Stringer was forgotten, the British Government was forgotten, contracts, hotel bills, steerage journeys to the States, all these were forgotten. The warmth, the sumptuous rooms, and the golden lamps of the " Savoy " were sufficient for the moment, and, as he sank into an easy chair and lit a cigarette, even his interest in the stranger and what he had to say was for a moment dimmed and diminished by the fumes that filled his brain and the ease that lapped his senses.

" What I have to say is this," said the stranger, leaning forward in his chair. " When I saw you here some time ago, I recognized you at once as a person I knew, but, as you put it, I could not place you. But when I got into the main hall a mirror at once told me. You are, to put it frankly, my twin image."

" I beg your pardon," said Jones, the word image shattering his complacency. " Your twin which, do you say ? "

" Image, likeness, counterpart. I mean no offence ; turn round and glance at that mirror behind you."

Jones did, and saw the stranger, and the stranger was himself. Both men belonged to a fairly common type, but the likeness went far beyond that—they were identical. The same hair and colour of hair, the same features, shape of head, eyes and colour of eyes, the same serious expression of countenance.

Absolute likeness between two human beings is almost as rare as absolute likeness between two pebbles on a beach, yet it occurs, as in the case of M. de Joinville and others well known and confirmed, and when I say absolute likeness, I mean likeness so complete that a close acquaintance cannot distinguish the difference between the duplicates. When Nature does a trick like this, she does it thoroughly, for it has been noticed—but more especially in the case of twins—that the likeness includes the voice, or, at least, its timbre, the thyroid cartilage and vocal chords following the mysterious law that rules the duplication.

Jones's voice and the voice of the stranger might have been the same, the only difference was in the accent, and that was slight.

" Well, I'm d——d," said Jones.

He turned to the other and then back to the mirror.

" Extraordinary, isn't it ? " said the other. " I don't know whether I ought to apologize to you or you to me. My name is Rochester."

Jones turned from the mirror, the two champagne cocktails, the whisky and the sherry were accommodating his unaccustomed brain to support this most unaccustomed situation. The thing seemed to him radiantly humorous, yet, if he had known it, there was very little humour in the matter.

" We must celebrate this," said Jones, calling an attendant and giving him explicit orders as to the means.

CHAPTER III

DINNER AND AFTER

A SMALL bottle of Bollinger was the means, and the celebration was mostly done by Jones, for it came about that this stranger, Rochester, whilst drinking little himself, managed by some method to keep up in gaiety and inconsequence of mind with the other, though every now and then he would fall away from the point, as a ship without a steersman falls away from the wind, and lapse for a moment into what an acute observer might have deemed to be the fundamental dejection of his real nature.

However, these lapses were only momentary, and did not interfere at all with the gay spirits of his companion, who, having found a friend in the midst of the loneliness of London, and his twin image in the person of that friend, was now pouring out his heart on every sort of subject, always returning, and with the regularity of a pendulum, to the fact of the likeness, and the same question and statement.

" What's this, your name ?   Rochester !   Well, 'pon my soul, this beats me."

Presently, the Bollinger finished, Jones found himself outside the " Savoy " with this new-found friend, walking in the gaslit Strand, and then, without any transition rememberable, he found himself seated at dinner in a private room of a French restaurant in Soho.

Afterwards he could remember parts of that dinner quite distinctly. He could remember the chicken and salad, and a rum omelette, at which he had laughed, because it was on fire. He could remember Rochester's gaiety, and a practical joke of some sort played on the waiter by Rochester, and ending in smashed plates ; he could remember remonstrating with the latter over his wild conduct. These things came to him afterwards, and also a few others—a place like Heaven, which was the Leicester Lounge, and a place like the other place, which was Leicester Square.

A quarrel with a stranger, about what he could not tell, a taxi-cab, in which he was seated listening to Rochester's voice giving directions to the driver, minute directions as to where he, Jones, was to be driven.

A lamp-lit hall and stairs up which he was being led. Nothing more.

CHAPTER IV

THE AWAKENING

HE awoke from sleep in bed in the dark, with his mind clear as crystal, and hot shame clutching at his throat. Rochester was the first recollection that came to him, and it was a recollection tinged with evil. Led by Rochester, he had made a fool of himself, he had made a brute of himself. How would he face the hotel people? And what had he done with the last of his money?

These thoughts held him motionless for a few terrific moments. Then he clapped his hand to his unfortunate head, turned on his side, and lay gazing into the darkness. It had all come back to him clearly.

Rochester's wild conduct, the dinner, the smashed plates, the quarrel. He was afraid to get up and search in his pockets; he guessed their condition. He occupied himself instead, trying to imagine what would become of him without money and without friends in this wilderness of London. With ten pounds he might have done something—without, what could he do? Nothing, unless it were manual labour, and he did not know where to look for that.

Then Rochester, never from his mind, came more fully before him—that likeness, was it real, or only a delusion of alcohol ?   And what else had Rochester done ?   He seemed mad enough to have done anything, plumb crazy.   Would he (Jones) be held accountable for Rochester's deeds ?   He was fighting with this question when a clock began to strike in the darkness close to the bed, nine delicate and silvery strokes, that brought a sudden sweat upon the forehead of Jones.

He was not in his room at the " Savoy."   There was no clock in the " Savoy " bedroom, and no clock in any hotel ever spoke in tones like these.   On the last stroke, and as if from a passage outside, he heard a voice :

" Took all his money and sent him home in another chap's clothes."

Then came the sound of a soft step crossing the carpet, the sound of curtain-rings moving, then a blind upshrivelled, letting the light of day upon a room never before seen by Jones—a Jacobean bedroom, severe but exquisite in every detail.

The man who had pulled the blind-string, and whose powerful profile was silhouetted against the light, showed to the sun a face highly but evenly coloured, as though by the gentle painting of old port wine through a long series of years and ancestors. The typical colour of the old-fashioned English judge, bishop and butler.

He was attired in a black morning-coat, and his whole countenance, make, build and appearance had something grave and archiepiscopal most holding to the eye and imagination.

It terrified Jones, who, breathing now as though asleep, watched through closed eyelids whilst the apparition, with pursed lips, dealt with the blind of the other window.

This done, it passed to the door, conferred in mute tones with some unseen person, and return d bearing in its hands a porcelain early morning tea-service.

Having placed this on the table by the bed, the apparition vanished, closing the door.

Jones sat up and looked around him.

His clothes had disappeared. He always hung his trousers on the bedpost at the end of his bed, and placed his other things on a chair; but trousers or other things were nowhere visible, they had been spirited away. It was at this moment that he noticed the gorgeous silk pyjamas he had got on. He held out his arm and looked at the texture and pattern.

Then in a flash came comfort and understanding. He was in Rochester's house. Rochester must have sent him here last night. That apparition was Rochester's manservant. The vision of Rochester turned from an evil spirit to an angel, and, filled with a warm sensation of friendliness towards the said Rochester, he was in the act of pouring out a cup of tea when the words he had heard spoken in the passage outside came back to him.

" Took all his money and sent him home in another chap's clothes."

What did that mean ?

He finished pouring out the tea and drank it ; there was thin bread and butter on a plate, but he disregarded it. Whose money had been taken, and who had been sent home in another chap's clothes ?

Did those words apply to him or to Rochester ? Had Rochester been robbed, might he (Jones) be held accountable ?

A deep uneasiness, and a passionate desire for his garments, begotten of these queries, brought him out of bed and on to the floor. He came to the nearer

2

window and looked out. The window gave upon St. James' Park, a cheerful view beneath the sky of a perfect summer's morning. He turned from the window, and, crossing the room, opened the door through which the apparition had vanished.

A thickly carpeted corridor lay outside, a corridor silent as the hypogeum of the Apis, secretive, gorgeous, with tasselled silk curtains and hanging lamps. Jones judged these lamps to be of silver, and worth a thousand dollars apiece. He had read the " Arabian Nights " when a boy, and, like a waft now from the garden of Aladdin, came a vague something stirring his senses and disturbing his practical nature. He wanted his clothes. This silent gorgeour had raised the desire for his garments to a passion. He wanted to get into his boots and face the world, and face the worst. Swinging lamps of silver, soft carpets, silken curtains, only served to heighten his sensitiveness as to his apparel and whole position.

He came back into the room. His anger was beginning to rise, the nervous anger of a man who has made a fool of himself, upon whom a jest is being played, and who finds himself in a false position.

Seeing an electric button by the fireplace, he went to it and pressed it twice, hard, then he opened the second door of the room and found a bathroom.

A Pompeian bathroom with tessellated floor, marble walls and marble ceiling. The bath was sunk in the floor. Across hot-water pipes, plated with silver, hung towels of huckaback, white towels with cardinal-red fringes. Here, too, most un-Pompeian, stood a wonderful dressing-table, one solid slab of glass, with razors set out, manicure instruments, brushes, pomade-pots, scent-bottles.

Jones came into this place, walked round it like a

cat in a strange larder, gauged the depth of the bath, glanced at the things on the table, and was in the act of picking up one of the manicure implements when a sound from the bedroom drew his attention.

Someone was moving about there. Someone who seemed altering the position of chairs and arranging things.

He judged it to be the servant who had answered the bell ; he considered that it was better to have the thing out now and have done with it. He wanted a full explanation, and bravely, but with the feelings of a man who is entering a dental parlour, he came to the bathroom door.

A pale-faced, agile-looking young man with glossy black hair, a young man in a sleeved-waistcoat, a young man carrying a shirt and set of pink silk under-garments over his left arm, was in the act of placing a pair of patent-leather boots with kid tops upon the floor. A gorgeous dressing-gown lay upon the bed. It had evidently been placed there by the agile one.

Jones had intended to ask explanations. That intention shrivelled somehow in the act of speech. What he uttered was a very mildly framed request.

" Er—can I have my clothes, please ? " said Jones.

" Yes, my lord," replied the other. " I am placing them out."

The instantaneous anger raised by the patent fact that he was being guyed by the second apparition was as instantly checked by the recollection of Rochester. Here was another practical joke. This house was evidently Rochester's—the whole thing was plain. Well, he would show that tricky spirit how he could take a joke and turn it on the maker. Like Brer Rabbit, he determined to lie low.

He withdrew into the bathroom, and sat down on the rush-bottomed chair by the table, his temper coiled and ready to fly' out like a spring. He was seated like this, curling his toes and nursing his resolve, when the agile one, with an absolute gravity that disarmed all anger, entered with the dressing-gown. He stood holding it up, and Jones, rising, put it on. Then the A.O. filled the bath, trying the temperature with a thermometer, and so absorbed in his business that he might have been alone.

The bath filled, he left the room, closing the door.

He had thrown some crystals into the water, scenting it with a perfume fragrant and refreshing ; the temperature was just right, and as Jones plunged and wallowed and lay half-floating, supporting himself by the silver-plated rails arranged for that purpose, the idea came to him that if the practical joke were to continue as pleasantly as it had begun, he, for one, would not grumble.

Soothed by the warmth, his mind took a clearer view of things.

If this were a jest of Rochester's, as most certainly it was, where lay the heart of it ? Every joke has its core, and the core of this one was most evidently the likeness between himself and Rochester.

If Rochester were a lord, and if this were his house, and if Rochester had sent him (Jones) home like a bundle of goods, then the extraordinary likeness would perhaps deceive the servants, and, maybe, other people as well. That would be a good joke, promising all sorts of funny developments. Only, it was not a joke that any man of self-respect would play. But Rochester, from those vague recollections of his antics, did not seem burdened with self-respect. He seemed in his latter developments crazy enough for anything.

If he had done this, then the servants were not in the business ; they would be under the delusion that he (Jones) was Rochester, doped and robbed, and dressed in another man's clothes and sent home.

Rochester, turning up later in the morning, would have a fine feast of humour to sit down to.

This seemed plain. The born practical joker, coming on his own twin image, could not resist making use of it. This explanation cleared the situation, but it did not make it a comfortable one. If the servants discovered the imposition before the arrival of Rochester, things would be unpleasant. He must act warily, get downstairs and escape from the place as soon as possible. Later on he would settle with Rochester. The servants, if they were not partners in the joke, had taken him on his face value ; his voice had evidently not betrayed him. He felt sure on this point. He left the bath, and drying himself, donned the dressing-gown. Tooth-paste and a tooth-brush stood on a glass tray by a little basin furnished with hot and cold water taps, and now, so strangely are men constituted, the main facts of his position were dwarfed for a second by the consideration that he had no tooth-brush of his own.

Just that little thing brought his energies to a focus and his growing irritation.

He opened the bedroom door. The glossy-haired one was putting links in the sleeves of a shirt.

" Get me a tooth-brush—a new one," said Jones brusquely, almost brutally. " Get it quick ! "

" Yes, my lord."

He dropped the shirt and left the room swiftly, but not hurriedly, taking care to close the door softly behind him.

It was the first indication to Jones of a method so

complete and a mechanism so perfectly constituted that jolts were all but eliminated.

" I believe if I'd asked that guy for an elephant," he said to himself, " he'd have acted just the same. Do they keep a drug-store on the premises ? "

They evidently kept a store of tooth-brushes, for in less than a minute and a half Expedition had returned with the tooth-brush on a little lacquered tray.

Now, to a man accustomed to dress himself, it comes as a shock to have his under-pants held out for him to get into as though he were a little boy.

This happened to Jones—and they were pink silk.

A pair of subfusc-coloured trousers, creased and looking absolutely new, were presented to him in the same manner. He was allowed to put on his own socks —silk and never worn before—but he was not allowed to put on his own boots. The perfect valet did that, kneeling before him shoe-horn and buttonhook in hand.

Having inducted him into a pink silk under-vest and a soft-pleated shirt, with plain gold links in the sleeves, each button of the said links having in its centre a small black pearl, a collar, and a subfusc-coloured silk tie were handed to him, also a black morning vest, and a black morning coat with rather broad braid at the edges.

A handkerchief of pure white cambric, with a tiny monogram in white, was then shaken out and presented.

Then his valet, intent, silent and seeming to move by clockwork, passed to a table on which stood a small oak cabinet ; opening the cabinet, he took from it and placed on the table a watch and chain.

His duties were now finished, and, according to some prescribed rule, he left the room carefully and softly, closing the door behind him.

Jones took up the watch and chain.

The watch was as thin as a five-shilling piece, the chain was a mere thread of gold. It was an evening affair, to be worn with dress clothes, and this fact presented to the mind of Jones a confirmation of the idea that not only was he literally in Rochester's shoes, but that Rochester's ordinary watch and chain had not returned.

He sat down for a moment to consider another point. His own old Waterbury and rolled gold chain, and the few unimportant letters in his pockets—where were they ?

He determined to clear this matter at once, and boldly rang the bell.

The valet answered it.

" When I came back last night—er—was there anything in my pockets ? " asked he.

" No, my lord. They had taken everything from the pockets."

" No watch and chain ? "

" No, my lord."

" Have you the clothes I came back in ? "

" Yes, my lord."

" Go and fetch them."

The man disappeared, and returned in a minute with a bundle of clothes neatly folded on his arm.

" Mr. Church told me to keep them careful, lest you'd want to put the matter in the hands of the police, my lord ; shockin' old things they are."

Jones examined the things. They were his own. Everything he had worn yesterday lay there, and the sight of them filled his mind with a nostalgia and a desire for them—a home-sickness and a clothes-sickness—beyond expression.

He was absolutely sure from the valet's manner

that the servants were not " in the know." A wild
impulse came to him to take the exhibitor of these
remnants of his past into his confidence. To say out :
" I'm Jones—Victor Jones, of Philadelphia. I'm no
lord. Gimme those clothes and let me out of this—
let's call it quits ! "

The word " Police " already dropped held him back.
He was an impostor—innocent enough, it is true,
but still an impostor. If he were to declare the facts
before Rochester returned, what might be the result ?
Whatever the result might be, one thing was certain—
it would be unpleasant. Besides, he was no prisoner ;
once downstairs he could leave the house.

So, instead of saying, " I'm Victor Jones, of Philadelphia," he said, " Take them away." And finding
himself alone once more, he sat down to consider.

Rochester must have gone through his pockets, not
for loot, but for the purpose of removing any article
that might cast suspicion, or raise the suspicion that
he (Jones) was not Rochester. That seemed plain
enough, and there was an earnestness of purpose in
the fact that was disturbing.

There was no use in thinking, however. He would
go downstairs and make his escape. He was savagely
hungry, but he reckoned the " Savoy " was good enough
for one meal—if he could get there.

Leaving the watch and chain—unambitious to add
a charge of larceny to his other troubles, should Fate
arrest him before the return of Rochester—he came
down the corridor to a landing giving upon a flight of
stairs, up which, save for the gradient, a coach and
horses might have been driven.

The place was a palace. Vast pictures by gloomy
old artists, pictures of men in armour, men in ruffs,
women without armour or ruffs, or even a rag of

chiffon, pictures worth millions of dollars, no doubt, hung from the walls of the landing and the wall flanking that triumphant staircase.

Jones looked over into the well of the hall, then he began to descend the stairs.

He had intended, on finding a hat in the hall, to clap it on and make a clean bolt for freedom and the light of heaven, get back to the " Savoy," dress himself in another suit, and, once more himself, go for Rochester ; but this was no hall with a hat-rack and umbrella-stand. Knights in armour were guarding it, and a flunkey six feet high, in red plush breeches and with calves that would have made Victor Jones scream with laughter under normal conditions.

The flunkey, seeing our friend, stepped to a door, opened it, and held it open for him. Not to enter the room thus indicated would have been possible enough, but the compelling influence of that vast flunkey made it impossible to Jones.

His volition had fled, he was subdued to his surroundings, for the moment, conquered.

He entered a breakfast-room, light and pleasantly furnished, where, at a breakfast-table and before a silver tea-urn, sat a lady of forty or so, thin-faced, high-nosed, aristocratic, and rather faded.

She was reading a letter, and when she saw the incomer she rose from the table and gathered some other letters up. Then she literally swept from the room. She looked at him as she passed, and it seemed to Jones that he had never known before the full meaning of the word " scorn."

For a wild second he thought that all had been discovered, that the police were now sure to arrive. Then he knew at once. Nothing had been discovered ; the delusion held even for this woman. That glance was meant for Rochester, not for him, and was caused by the affair of last night ; by other things too, maybe, but that surely.

Uncomfortable, angry, nervous, wild to escape, and then yielding to caution, he took his seat at the table where a place was laid, evidently for him.

The woman had left an envelope on the table ; he glanced at it.

> " Lady Venetia Birdbrook,
>   " 10A, Carlton House Terrace,
>   " London, S.W."

Victor read the inscription, written in a bold, female hand.

It told him where he was. He was in the breakfast-room of 10A, Carlton House Terrace, but it told him nothing more.

Was Lady Venetia Birdbrook his wife, or, at least, the wife of his twin image ? This thought blinded him for a moment to the fact that a flunkey—they seemed as numerous as flies in May—was at his elbow asking him would he have kippers or scrambled eggs, whilst another flunkey, who seemed to have sprung from the floor, was fiddling at the sideboard, which contained cold edibles—tongue, ham, chicken, and so forth.

" Scrambled eggs," said he.

" Tea or coffee, my lord ? "

" Coffee."

He broke a breakfast roll and helped himself mechanically to some butter, which was instantly presented to him by the sideboard fiddler, and he had just taken a mechanical bite of buttered roll when the door opened, and the archiepiscopal gentleman who had pulled up his window blind that morning entered.

Mr. Church—for Jones had already gathered that to be his name—carried a little yellow basket filled with letters in his right hand, and in his left a great sheaf—the *Times*, *Daily Telegraph*, *Morning Post*, *Daily Mail*, *Daily Express*, *Chronicle* and *Daily News*. These papers he placed on a side table evidently intended for that purpose. The little letter-basket he placed on the table at Jones's left elbow.

Then he withdrew, but not without having spoken a couple of murmured words of correction to the flunkey near the sideboard, who had omitted, no doubt, some point in the mysterious ritual of which he was an acolyte.

Jones glanced at the topmost letter.

" The Earl of Rochester,
        " 10A, Carlton House Terrace,
                " London, S.W."

Ah, now he knew it ! The true name of the juggler who had played him this trick. It was plain, too, now, that Rochester had sent him here as a substitute.

But the confirmation of his idea did not ease his mind. On the contrary, it filled him with a vague alarm. The feeling of being in a trap came upon him now for the first time. The joke had lost any semblance of colour, the thing was serious. Rochester ought to have been back to put an end to the business before this. Had anything happened to him ? Had he got gaoled ?

He did not touch the letters. Without raising suspicion, acting as naturally as possible the part of a peer of the realm, he must escape as swiftly as possible from this nest of flunkeys, and with that object in view he accepted the scrambled eggs now presented to him, and the coffee.

When they were finished, he rose from the table. Then he remembered the letters. Here was another tiny tie. He could not leave them unopened and untouched on the table without raising suspicion. He took them from the basket, and with them in his hand left the room, the fellow in waiting slipping before to open the door.

The hall was deserted, for a wonder, deserted by all but the men in armour. A room where he might leave the infernal letters, and find a bell to fetch a servant to get him a hat, was the prime necessity of the moment.

He crossed to a door directly opposite, opened it, and found a room, half-library, half-study, a pleasant room used to tobacco, with a rather well-worn Turkey carpet on the floor, saddle-bag easy-chairs, and a great escritoire in the window, open and showing pigeon-holes containing notepaper, envelopes, telegraph forms, and a rack containing the " A B C Railway Guide," " Whitaker's Almanac," " Ruff's Guide to the Turf," " Who's Who," and " Kelly."

Pipes were on the mantelpiece, a silver cigar-box and cigarette-box on a little table by one of the easy-chairs, matches—nothing was here wanting, and everything was of the best.

He placed the letters on the table, opened the cigar-box, and took from it a Roman Alones—a blunt-ended weapon for the destruction of melancholy and unrest, four and a half inches long, and costing perhaps half a crown—a real Havana cigar. Now, in London there are only four places where you can obtain a real and perfect Havana cigar—that is to say, four shops. And at those four shops—or shall we call them emporiums ?—only known and trusted customers can find the sun that shone on the Vuelta Abajos in such and such a perfect year.

The Earl of Rochester's present representative was finding it now, with little enough pleasure, however, as he paced the room preparatory to ringing the bell. He was approaching the electric button for this purpose, when the faint and faraway murmuring of an automobile, as if admitted by a suddenly opened hall door, checked his hand. Here was Rochester at last. He waited listening.

He had not long to wait.

The door of the room suddenly opened, and the woman of the breakfast-table disclosed herself. She was dressed for going out, wearing a hat that seemed a yard in diameter, and a feather boa, from which her hen-like face and neck rose to the crowning triumph of the hat.

" I am going to mother," said she. " I am not coming back."

" Um-um," said Jones.

She paused. Then she came right in and closed the door behind her.

Standing with her back close to the door she spoke to Jones.

" If you cannot see your own conduct as others see it, who can make you ? I am not referring to the disgrace of last night, though, Heaven knows that was bad enough. I am talking of *everything*, of your poor wife, who loves you still, of the estate you have ruined by your lunatic conduct, of the company you keep, of the insults you have heaped on people—and now you add drink to the rest. That's new." She paused. " That's new. But I warn you, your brain won't stand *that*. You know the taint in the family as well as I do ; it has shown itself in your actions ; well, go on drinking and you will end in Bedlam instead of the workhouse. They call you ' Mad Rochester,' you know that." She choked. " I have blushed to be known as your sister. I have tried to keep my place here and save you. It's ended."

She turned to the door.

Jones had been making up his mind. He would tell the whole affair. This Rochester was a thorough bad lot, evidently ; well, he would turn the tables on him now.

" Look here," said he. " I am not the man you think I am."

" Tosh ! " cried the woman.

She opened the door, passed out, and shut it with a snap.

" Well, I'm d——d," said Jones, for the second time in connection with Rochester.

The clock on the mantelpiece pointed to quarter to eleven, the faint sound of the car had ceased. The lady of the feather boa had evidently taken her departure, and the house had resumed its cloistral silence.

He waited a moment to make sure, then he went into the hall where a huge flunkey—a new one, more curious than the others—was lounging near the door.

" My hat," said Jones.

The thing flew, and returned with a glossy silk hat, a tortoiseshell-handled cane, and a pair of new suède gloves of a delicate dove colour. Then it opened the door, and Jones, clapping the hat on his head, walked out.

The hat fitted, by a mercy.

CHAPTER V

THE POINT OF THE JOKE

OUT in the open air and sunshine, he took a deep, satisfying breath. He felt as though he had escaped from a cage full of monkeys. Monkeys in the form of men, creatures who would servilely obey him as Rochester, but who, scenting the truth, would rend him in pieces.

Well, he was clear of them. Once back in the " Savoy " he would get into his own things, and once in his own things he would strike. If he could not get a lawyer to take his case up against Rochester, he would go to the police. Yes, he would. Rochester had doped him, taken his letters, taken his watch.

Jones was not the man to bring false charges ; he knew that in taking his belongings, this infernal jester had done so, not for plunder, but for the purpose of making the servants believe that he, Rochester, had been stripped of everything by sharks, and sent home in an old suit of clothes ; all the same, he would charge Rochester with the taking of his things—he would teach this practical joker how to behave.

To cool himself and collect his thoughts before going to the " Savoy " he took a walk in St. James' Park.

That one word " Tosh ! " uttered by the woman, in

answer to what he had said, told him more about Rochester than many statements. This man wanted a cold bath, he wanted to be held under the tap till he cried for mercy.

Walking, now with the stick under his right arm and his left hand in his trousers-pocket, he felt something in the pocket. It was a coin. He took it out. It was a penny, undiscovered evidently, and unremoved by the valet.

It was also a reminder of his own poverty-stricken condition. His thoughts turned from Rochester and his jokes to his own immediate and tragic position. The whole thing was his own fault. It was quite easy to say that Rochester had led him along and tempted him ; he was a full-grown man, and should have resisted temptation. He had let strong drink get hold of him ; well, he had paid by the loss of his money, to say nothing of the way his self-respect had been bruised by this jester.

Near Buckingham Palace he turned back, walking by the way he had come, and leaving the park at the new gate.

He crossed the plexus of ways where Northumberland Avenue debouches on Trafalgar Square. It was near twelve o'clock, and the first evening papers were out. A hawker with a bundle of papers under his arm and a yellow poster in front of him like an apron, drew his attention, at least the poster did.

"Suicide of an American in London," were the words on the poster.

Jones, remembering his penny, produced it, and bought a paper.

The American's suicide did not interest him, but he fancied vaguely that something of Rochester's doings of the night before might have been caught by the Press through the police news. He thought it highly probable that Rochester, continuing his mad course, had been gaoled.

He was rewarded. Right on the first page he saw his own name. He had never seen it before in print, and the sight and the circumstance made his tongue cluck back, as though chucked by a string tied to its root.

This was the paragraph.

" Last night, as the 11.30 Inner Circle train was entering the Temple Station, a man was seen to jump from the platform on to the metals. Before the station officials could interfere to save him, the unfortunate man had thrown himself before the incoming engine. Death was instantaneous.

" From papers in possession of deceased, his identity has been verified as that of Mr. V. A. Jones, an American gentleman of Philadelphia, lately resident at the Savoy Hotel, Strand."

Jones stood with the paper in his hand, appalled. Rochester had committed suicide !

This was the jest—the black core of it. All last evening, all through that hilarity he had been plotting this. Plotting it perhaps from the first moment of their meeting. Unable to resist the prompting of the extraordinary likeness, this joker, this waster, done to the world, had left life at the end of a last jamboree, and with a burst of laughter—leaving another man in his clothes, nay, almost one might say, in his body

Jones saw the point of the thing at once.

PART II

CHAPTER I

THE NET

HE saw something else. He was automatically barred from the " Savoy," and barred from the American Consul. And, on top of that, something else. He had committed a very grave mistake in accepting for a moment his position. He should have spoken at once that morning, spoken to " Mr. Church," told his tale and made explanations ; failing that, he should have made explanations before leaving the house. He had left in Rochester's clothes, he had acted the part of Rochester.

He rolled the paper into a ball, tossed it into the gutter, and entered Charing Cross Station to continue his soliloquy.

He had eaten Rochester's food, smoked one of his cigars, accepted his cane and gloves. All that might have been explainable with Rochester's aid, but Rochester was dead.

No one knew that Rochester was dead. To go back to the " Savoy " and establish his own identity, he would have to establish the fact of Rochester's death, tell the story of his own intoxication, and make people believe that he was an innocent victim.

An innocent victim who had gone to another man's house, and palpably masqueraded for some hours as

34

that other man, walking out of the house in his clothes and carrying his stick, an innocent victim, who owed a bill at the "Savoy."

Why, every man, the family included, you may be sure, would be finding the innocent victim in Rochester.

What were Jones's letters doing on Rochester ? That was a nice question for a puzzle-headed jury to answer.

By what art did Jones, the needy American adventurer—that was what they would call him—impose himself upon Rochester, and induce Rochester to order him to be taken to Carlton House Terrace ?

Oh, there were a lot more questions to be asked at that phantom court of justice, where Jones beheld himself in the dock trying to explain the inexplicable.

The likeness would not be any use for white-washing ; it would only deepen the mystery, make the affair more extravagant. Besides, the likeness most likely by this would be pretty well spoiled ; by the time of the assizes it would be only verifiable by photographs.

Sitting on a seat in Charing Cross Station, he cogitated thus, chasing the most fantastic ideas, yet gripped all the time by the cold fact.

The fact that the only door in London open to him was the door of 10A, Carlton House Terrace.

Unable to return to the "Savoy," he possessed nothing in the world but the clothes he stood up in, and the walking-stick he held in his hand. Dressed like a lord, he was poorer than any tramp, for the simple reason that his extravagantly fine clothes barred him from begging, and from the menial work that is the only recourse of the suddenly destitute.

Given time, and with his quick business capacity, he might have made a fight to obtain a clerkship, or some post in a store—but he had no time. It was

3*

near the luncheon hour, and he was hungry. That fact alone was an indication of how he was placed as regards time.

He was a logical man. He saw clearly that only two courses lay before him. To go to the "Savoy" and tell his story and get food and lodging in the police station, or to go to 10A, Carlton House Terrace and get food and lodging as Rochester.

Both ideas were hateful, but he reckoned, and with reason, that if he took the first course, arrest and ignominy, and probably imprisonment, would be certain, whereas if he took the second he might be able to bluff the thing out till he could devise means of escape from the net that surrounded him.

He determined on the second course. The servants, and even that scarecrow woman in the feather boa, had accepted him as good coin, there was no reason why they should not go on accepting him for a while. For the matter of that, there was no reason why they should not go on accepting him for ever.

Even in the midst of his disturbance of mind and general tribulation, the humour of the latter idea almost made him smile. The idea of living and dying as Lord Rochester, as a member of the English aristocracy, always being "my lorded," served by flunkeys with big calves, and inducted every morning into his under-pants by that guy in the sleeved jacket.

This preposterous idea, more absurd than any dream, was yet based on a substantive foundation. In fact, he had that morning put it in practice, and unless a miracle occurred he would have to continue putting it in practice for some days to come.

However, Jones, fortunately or unfortunately for himself, was a man of action and no dreamer. He dismissed the idea and came to practical considerations.

If he had to hold on to the position, he would have to make more sure of his ground.

He rose, found his way into Charing Cross Station Hotel, and obtained a copy of " Who's Who," from the hotel clerk.

He turned the pages till he found the R's. Here was his man.

" Rochester, 21 Earl of (cr. 1431), Arthur Coningsby Delamere. Baron Coningsby of Wilton, ex-Lieut., Rifle Brigade. M. Teresa, 2nd daughter of Sir Peter Mason, Bart., *q.v.* Educ. Heidelberg. Owns about 21,000 acres. Address : 10A, Carlton House Terrace. Rochester Court, Rochester. The Hatch, Colney, Wilts. Clubs : Senior Conservative, National Sporting, Pelican."

That was only a part of the sayings of " Who's Who " regarding Rochester, Arthur Coningsby Delamere, the last decadent descendant of a family that had been famous in long past years for its power, prodigality, and profligacy.

If Jones could have climbed up his own family tree he might have found on some distaff branch the reason of his appalling likeness to Rochester, Arthur Coningsby Delamere, but that is a pure matter of speculation, and it did not enter the mind of Jones.

He closed the book, returned it, and walked out.

Now that his resolve was made, his fighting spirit was roused. In other words, he felt the same recklessness that a man feels who is going into battle, the disregardlessness of consequence, which marks your true explorer. For Stanley on the frontier of Darkest Africa, Scott on the ice-rim of the Beardmore Glacier, had before them positions and districts simple in comparison to those that now fronted Jones, who had

before him the western and south-western London
districts, with all they contained in the way of natives
in top-hats, natives painted and powdered, tribes with
tribal laws of which he knew little, tricks of which he
knew less, convenances, jujus and fetishes.   And he
was entering this dark, intricate, and dangerous
country, not as an explorer, carrying beads and Bibles,
but disguised as a top man, a chief.

Burton's position when he journeyed to Mecca, disguised as a Mohammedan, was easy compared to the
position of Jones. Burton knew the ritual. He
made one mistake in it, it is true, but then he was able
to kill the man who saw him make that mistake.
Jones could not protect himself in this way, even if
the valet in the sleeved jacket were to discover him
in a position analogous to Burton's.

He was not thinking of any of these things at the
present moment, however, he was thinking of luncheon.
If he were condemned to play the part of a lord for
awhile, he was quite determined to take his salary in
the way of everything he wanted. Yet it seemed that
to obtain anything he wanted in his new and extraordinary position he would have to take something he
did not want. He wanted luncheon, but he did not
want to go back to Carlton House Terrace—at least, not
just now. Those flunkeys—the very thought of them
gave him indigestion ; more than that, he was afraid
of them. A fear that was neither physical nor moral,
but more in the nature of the fear of women for mice,
or the supposed fear of the late Lord Roberts for cats.

The solemn Church, the mercurial valet, the men
with calves, belonged to a tribe that, maybe, had
done Jones to death in some past life, either bored him
to death or bludgeoned him ; it did not matter, the
antipathy was there, and it was powerful.

At the corner of Northumberland Avenue an idea
came to him. This Rochester belonged to several
clubs—why not go and have luncheon at one of them
on credit ? It would save him for the moment from
returning to the door towards which Fate was shepherding him, and he might be able to pick up some
extra wrinkles about himself and his position. The
idea was indicative of the daring of the man, though
there was little enough danger in it. He was sure of
passing muster at a club, since he had done so at home.
He carried the names of two of Rochester's clubs in
his mind—the Pelican and the Senior Conservative.
The latter seemed the more stodgy, the least likely
to offer surprises in the way of shoulder-clapping,
irresponsible parties who might want to enter into
general conversation.

He chose it, asked a policeman for directions, and
made for Pall Mall.

Here another policeman pointed out to him the
building he was in search of.

It stood on the opposite side of the way, a building
of grey stone, vast and serious of feature, yet opulent
and hinting of the best in all things relative to comfort.

It was historical. Disraeli had come down those
steps, and the great Lord Salisbury had gone up them.
Men to enter this place had to be born not made, and
even these selected ones had to put their names
down at birth, if they wished for any chance of lunch-
ing there before they lost their teeth and hair.

It took twenty-one years for the elect to reach this
place, and on the way they were likely to be slain by
black balls.

Victor Jones just crossed the road and went up the
steps.

CHAPTER II

LUNCHEON

HE had lunched at the "Constitutional" with a chance acquaintance picked up on his first week in London, so he knew something of the ways of English clubs, yet the vast hall of this place daunted him for a moment.

However, the club servants seeming to know him, and recognizing that indecision is the most fatal weakness of man, he crossed the hall, and, seeing some gentlemen going up the great staircase, he followed to a door on the first landing.

He saw through the glass swing-doors that this was the great luncheon-room of the club, and, having made this discovery, he came downstairs again, where good fortune, in the form of a bald-headed man without hat or stick, coming through a passage way, indicated the cloak-room to him.

Here he washed his hands and brushed his hair, and, looking at himself in a glass, judged his appearance to be conservative and all right. He, a democrat of the democrats in this hive of aristocracy and old crusted conservatism, might have felt qualms of political conscience but for the fact that earthly politics, social theories, and social instincts were less to him now than to an inhabitant of the dark body that tumbles and fumbles around Sirius. Less than the difference between the minnow and the roach, to the roach in the landing-net.

Leaving the place, he almost ran into the arms of a gentleman who was entering, and who gave him a curt "'H' do!"

He knew that man. He had seen his newspaper portrait in America as well as England. It was the leader of his Majesty's Opposition, the queen bee of this hive where he was about to sit down to lunch. The queen bee did not seem very friendly, a fact that augured ill for the attitude of the workers and the drones.

Arrived at the glass swing-doors before mentioned, he looked in.

The place was crowded.

It looked to him as though, for the space of a mile and a half or so, lay tables, tables, tables, all occupied by twos and threes and fours of men. Conservative looking men, and, no doubt, mostly lords.

It was too late to withdraw, without shattering his own self-respect and self-confidence. The cold bath was before him, and there was no use putting a toe in.

He opened the door and entered, walking between the tables, and looking the luncheon parties in the face.

The man seated has a tremendous advantage over the man standing in this sort of game. One or two of the members met by the new-comer's glance bowed in the curious manner of the seated Briton, the eyes of others fell away, others nodded frigidly, it seemed to Jones. Then, like a pilot fish before a shark leading him to his food, a club waiter developed and piloted him to a small, unoccupied table, where he took a seat and looked at the menu handed to him by the pilot.

He ordered fillet of sole, roast chicken, salad, and

strawberry ice.   They were the easiest things to order.
He would have ordered roast elephant's trunk had it
been easier and on the menu.

A man after the storming of Hell Gate, or just
dismounted after the charge of the Light Brigade,
would have possessed as little instinct for menu-
hunting as Jones.

He had pierced the ranks of the British aristocracy
—that was nothing ; he was seated at their camp fire,
sharing their food, and they were all inimical towards
him—that was everything.

He felt the draught.   He felt that these men had
a down on him, felt it by all sorts of senses that seemed
newly developed.   Not a down on him (Jones) but a
down on him—Rochester, Arthur Coningsby Delamere, 21st Earl of.

And the extraordinary thing was that he felt it.
What on earth did it matter to him if these men looked
coldly upon another man ?   It did.   It mattered quite
a lot, more than, perhaps, it ever mattered to the other
man.   Is the soul such a shallow and blind thing that
it cannot sort the true from the false, the material
from the immaterial, see that an insult levelled at a
likeness is not an insult levelled at it ?

Surely not, and yet the soul of Victor Jones resented
the coolness of others towards the supposed body of
Rochester, as though it were a personal insult.

It was the first intimation to Jones that when the
actor puts on his part he puts on more than a cloak or
trunk hose, that the personality he had put on had
nerves curiously associated with his own nerves, and
that, though he might say to himself a hundred times
with respect to the attitudes of other people, " Pah !
they don't mean me ! " that formula was no charm
against disdain.

The wine butler, a gentleman not unlike Mr. Church, was now at his elbow, and he found himself contemplating the wine-card of the Senior Conservative, a serious document, if one may judge by the faces of the men who peruse it.

It is, in fact, the Almanach de Gotha of wines. The old kings of wine are here, the princes, and all the aristocracy. Unlike the Almanach de Gotha, however, the price of each is set down. Unlike the Almanach de Gotha, the names of a few commoners are admitted.

Macon was here, and even Blackways' cyder, the favourite tipple of the old Duke of Taunton.

Jones ran his eye over the list without enthusiasm. He had taken a dislike to alcohol even in its mildest guise.

" Er—what minerals have you got ? " asked he.

" Minerals ? "

The man with the wine-card was nonplussed. Jones saw his mistake.

" Soda-water," said he. " Get me some soda-water."

The fillet of sole with sauce Tartare was excellent. Nothing, not even the minerals could dim that fact. As he ate he looked about him, and with all the more ease, because he found now that nobody was looking at him, his self-consciousness died down, and he began speculating on the men around, their probable rank, fortune and intellect. It seemed to Jones that the latter factor was easier of determination than the other two.

What struck him more forcibly was a weird resemblance between them all, a phantom thing, a link undiscoverable yet somehow there. This tribal expression is one of the strangest phenomena eternally confronting and battering our senses.

Just as men grow like their wives, so do they grow like their fellow-tradesmen, waiters like waiters, grooms like grooms, lawyers like lawyers, politicians like politicians. More, it has been undeniably proved that landowners grow like landowners, just as shepherds grow like sheep, and aristocrats like aristocrats.

A common idea moulds faces to its shape, and a common want of ideas allows external circumstances to do the moulding.

So, English Conservative politicians of the higher order being worked upon by external circumstances of a similar nature, have perhaps a certain similar expression. Radical politicians, on the other hand, shape to a common idea—evil, but still an idea.

Jones was not thinking this, he was just recognizing that all these men belonged to the same class, and he felt in himself that not only did he not belong to that class, but that Rochester also, probably, had found himself in the same position by temperament.

That might have accounted for the wildness and eccentricity of Rochester, as demonstrated in that mad carouse, and hinted at by the woman in the feather boa. The wildness of a monkey condemned to live amongst goats, hanging on to their horns, and clutching at their scutts, and playing all the tricks that contrariness might suggest to a contrary nature.

Something of this sort was passing through Jones's mind, and, as he attacked his strawberry ice, for the first time since reading that momentous piece of news in the evening paper, his mental powers became focussed on the question that lay at the very heart of all this business. It struck him now so very forcibly that he laid down his spoon and stared before him, forgetful of the place where he was and the people around him.

" Why did that guy commit suicide ? "

That was the question.

He could find no answer to it.

A man does not, as a rule, commit suicide simply because he is eccentric or because he has made a mess of his estates, or because, being a practical joker, he suddenly finds his twin image to defraud. Rochester had evidently done nothing to bar him from society ; though perhaps coldly received by his club, he was still received by it. Had he done something that society did not know of, something that might suddenly obtrude itself ?

Jones was brought back from this reverie with a snap. One of the confounded waiters was making off with his half-eaten ice.

" Hi ! " cried he. " What you doing ? Bring that back ! "

His voice rang through the room, people turned to look. He mentally cursed the ice and the creature who had snapped it from him, finished it, devoured a wafer, and then, rising to his feet, left the room. It was easier to leave than to come in, other men were leaving, and in the general break up he felt less observed.

Downstairs he looked through glass doors into a room where men were smoking, correct men in huge arm-chairs, men with legs stretched out, men smoking big cigars and talking politics, no doubt. He wanted to smoke, but he did not want to smoke in that place.

He went to the cloak-room, fetched his hat and cane and gloves, and left the club.

Outside in Pall Mall he remembered that he had not told the waiter to credit him with the luncheon, but a trifle like that did not bother him now. They would be sure to put it down.

What did trouble him was the still unanswered question :

" Why did that guy commit suicide ? "

Suppose Rochester had murdered some man and had committed suicide to escape the consequences ? This thought gave him a cold grue such as he had never experienced before. For a moment he saw himself hauled before a British court of justice ; for a moment, and for the first time in his life, he found himself wondering what a hangman might be like.

But Victor Jones, though a visionary sometimes in business, was at base a business man. More used to his position now, and looking it fairly in the face, he found that he had little to fear even if Rochester had committed a murder. He could, if absolutely driven to it, prove his identity. Driven to it, he could prove his life in Philadelphia, bring witnesses and relate circumstances. His tale would all hang together, simply because it was the truth. This inborn assurance heartened him a lot, and, more cheerful now, he began to recognize more of the truth. His position was very solid. Everyone had accepted him. Unless he came an awful bump over some crime committed by the late defunct, he could go on for ever as the Earl of Rochester. He did not want to go on for ever as the Earl of Rochester. He wanted to get back to the States and just be himself, and he intended so to do, having scraped a little money together. But the idea tickled him just as it had done in Charing Cross Station, and it had lost its monstrous appearance, and had become humorous, a highly dangerous appearance for a dangerous idea to take.

Jones was a great walker, exercise always cleared his mind and strengthened his judgment. He set off on a long walk now, passing through Piccadilly to

Regent Circus, then up Regent Street and Oxford Street, and along Oxford Street towards the West. He found himself in High Street, Kensington, in Hammersmith, and then in those dismal regions where the country struggles with the town.

Oh, those suburbs of London! Within easy reach of the City! Those battalions of brick houses, bits of corpses of what once were fields, those villas, laundries!

The contrast between this place and Pall Mall came as a sudden revelation to Jones, the contrast between the power, ease, affluence and splendour of the surroundings of the Earl of Rochester and the surroundings of the bank clerks and small people who dwelt here.

The viewpoint is everything. From here Carlton House Terrace seemed almost pleasing.

Jones, like a good Democrat, had all his life professed a contempt for rank. Titles had seemed as absurb to him as feathers in a monkey's cap. It was here in ultra Hammersmith that he began to review this question from a more British standpoint.

Tell it not in Gath, he was beginning to feel the vaguest antipathetic stirring against little houses and ultra people.

He turned and began to retrace his steps. It was seven o'clock when he reached the door of 10A, Carlton House Terrace.

CHAPTER III

MR. VOLES

THE flunkey who admitted him, having taken his hat, stick, and gloves, presented him with a letter that had arrived by the midday post, also with a piece of information.

" Mr. Voles called to see you, my lord, shortly after twelve. He stated that he had an appointment with you. He is to call again at a quarter-past seven."

Jones took the letter and went with it to the room where he had sat that morning. Upon the table lay all the letters that he had not opened that morning. He had forgotten these. Here was a mistake. If he wished to hold to his position for even a few days, it would be necessary to guard against mistakes like this.

He hurriedly opened them, merely glancing at the contents, which for the most part were unintelligible to him.

There was a dinner invitation from Lady Snorries —whoever she might be—and a letter beginning " Dear old boy," from a female who signed herself " Julie " ; an appeal from a begging-letter writer, and a letter beginning " Dear Rochester," from a gentleman who signed himself simply " Childersley."

The last letter he opened was the one he had just received from the servant.

It was written on poor paper, and it ran :

" Stick to it—if you can.   You'll see why I couldn't. There's a fiver under the papers of the top right-hand drawer of bureau in smoke-room.

" ROCHESTER."

Jones knew that this letter, though addressed to the Earl of Rochester, was meant for him, and was written by Rochester, written probably on some bar counter, and posted at the nearest pillar-box just before he had committed the act.

He went to the drawer in the bureau indicated, raised the papers in it, and found a five-pound note.

Having glanced at it, he closed the drawer, placed the note in his waistcoat pocket, and sat down again at the table.

" Stick to it—if you can."   The words rang in his ears just as though he had heard them spoken.

Those words, backed by the five-pound note, wrought a great change in the mind of Jones. He had Rochester's permission to act as he was acting, and a little money to help in his actions.

The fact of his penury had been like a wet blanket upon him all day.   He felt that power had come to him with permission.   He could think clearly now. He rose and paced the floor.

" Stick to it—if you can ! "

Why not—why not—why not ?   He found himself laughing out loud.   A great gush of energy had come to him.   Jones was a man of that sort.   A new and great idea always came to him on the crest of a wave of energy.   The British Government Contract idea had come to him like that, and the wave had carried him to England.

4

Why not be the Earl of Rochester, make good his position finally, stand on the pinnacle where Fate had placed him, and carry this thing through to its ultimate issue ?

It would not be all jam. Rochester must have been very much pressed by circumstances. That did not frighten Jones. To him the game was everything, and the battle.

He would make good where Rochester had failed, meet the difficulties that had destroyed the other, face them, overcome them.

His position was unassailable.

Coming over from New York, he had read Nelson's shilling edition of the " Life of Sir Henry Hawkins." He had read with amazement the story of British credulity expressed in the Tichborne case. How Arthur Orton, a butcher, scarcely able to write, had imposed himself on the public as Roger Tichborne, a young aristocrat of good education.

He contrasted his own position with Orton's.

He was absolutely unassailable.

He went to the cigar-box, chose a cigar, and lit it.

There was the question of handwriting. That suddenly occurred to him, confronting his newly-formed plans. He would have to sign cheques, write letters. A typewriter could settle the latter question, and as for the signature, he possessed a sample of Rochester's, and would have to imitate it. At the worst he could pretend he had injured his thumb—that excuse would last some time.

" There's one big thing about the whole business," said he to himself, " and that is the chap's eccentricity. Why, if I'm shoved too hard, I can pretend to have lost my memory or my wits. There's not a blessed card I haven't either in my hand or up my sleeve, and if worst comes to worst, I can always prove my identity and tell my story."

He was engaged with thoughts like these when the door opened and the servant, bearing a card on a salver, announced that Mr. Voles, the gentleman who had called earlier in the day, had arrived.

" Bring him in," said Victor.

The servant retired, and returned immediately, ushering in Voles, who entered carrying his hat before him. The stranger was a man of fifty, a tubby man, dressed in a black frock coat, covered, despite the summer weather, by a thin black overcoat with silk facings. His face was evil, thick-skinned, yellow, heavy nosed ; the hair of the animal was jet black, thin, and presented to the eyes of the gazer a small Disraeli curl upon the forehead of the owner.

The card announced :

" MR. A. S. VOLES,
" 12b, *Jermyn Street."*

Voles himself, and unknown to himself, announced a lot of other things.

Victor Jones had a sharp instinct for men, well whetted by experience.

He nodded to the new-comer curtly, and without rising from his chair ; the servant shut the door, and the two men were alone.

Just as a dog's whole nature livens at the smell of a polecat, so did Jones's nature at the sight of Voles. He felt this man to be an enemy.

Voles came to the table and placed his hat upon it. Then he turned, went to the door and opened it to see if the servant was listening.

He shut the door.

4*

" Well," said he, " have you got the money for me ? "

Another man in Jones's position might have asked, and with reason, " What money ? "

Jones simply said " No."

This simple answer had a wonderful effect. Voles, about to take a seat, remained standing, clasping the back of the chair he had chosen. Then he burst out :

" You fooled me yesterday, and gave me an appointment for to-day. I called, you were out."

" Was I ? "

" Were you ? You said the money would be here waiting for me—well, here I am now. I've got a cab outside ready to take it."

" And suppose I don't give it to you ? " asked Jones.

" We won't suppose any nonsense like that," replied Voles, taking his seat ; " not so long as there is the law."

" That's true," said the other. " We don't want the law."

" You don't," replied Voles.

He was staring at Jones. The Earl of Rochester's voice struck him as not quite the same as usual ; more spring in it and vitality—altered, in fact. But he supposed nothing of the truth. Passed as good coin by Voles, Jones had nothing to fear from any man or woman in London, for the eye of Voles was unerring, the ear of Voles ditto, the mind of Voles balanced like a jeweller's scales.

" True," said Jones, " I don't. Well, let's talk about this money. Couldn't you take half to-night and half in a week's time ? "

" Not me," replied the other. " I must have the two thousand to-night, same as usual."

Jones had the whole case in his hands now, and he

began preparing the toast on which to put this most evident blackmailer when cooked.

His quick mind had settled everything. Here was the first obstacle in his path ; it would have to be destroyed, not surmounted. He determined to destroy it. If the worst came to the worst, if whatever crime Rochester had committed were to be pressed home on him by Voles, he would declare everything, prove his identity by sending for witnesses from the States, and show Rochester's letter. The blackmailing would account for Rochester's suicide.

But Jones knew blackmailers, and he knew that Voles would never prosecute. Rochester must indeed have been a weak fool not to have grasped this nettle and torn it up by the roots. He forgot that Rochester was probably guilty—that makes all the difference in the world.

" You shall have the money," said he. " But, see here, let's make an end of this. Now, let's see. How much have you had already ? "

" Only eight," said Voles. " You know that well enough, why ask ? "

" Eight thousand," murmured the other. " You have had eight thousand pounds out of me, and the two to-night will make ten. Seems a good price for a few papers."

He made the shot on spec. It was a bull's-eye.

" Oh, those papers are worth a good deal more than that," said Voles, " a good deal more than that."

So it was documents, not actions that the black-mailer held in suspense over the head of Rochester. It really did not matter a button to Jones ; he stood ready to face murder itself, armed as he was with Rochester's letter in his pocket, and the surety of being able to identify himself.

" Well," said he, " let's finish this business. Have
you a cheque-book on you ? "

" I have a cheque-book right enough. What's
your game now ? "

" Just an idea of mine before I pay you. Bring
out your cheque-book, you'll see what I mean in a
minute."

Voles hesitated, then, with a laugh, he took the
cheque-book from the breast-pocket of his overcoat.

" Now tear out a cheque."

" Tear out a cheque ! " cried the other. " What
on earth are you getting at—one of my cheques ?
This is good."

" Tear out a cheque," insisted the other ; " it will
only cost you a penny, and you will see my meaning
in a moment."

The animal, before the insistent direction of the
other, hesitated, then, with a laugh, he tore out a
cheque.

" Now place it on the table."

Voles placed it on the table.

Jones, going to the bureau, fetched pen and ink.
He pushed a chair to the table, and made the other sit
down.

" Now," said Jones, " write me out a cheque for
eight thousand pounds."

Voles threw down the pen with a laugh—it was
his last in that room.

" You won't ? " said Jones.

" Oh, quit this fooling ! " replied the other. " I've
no time for such stuff. What are you doing now ? "

" Ringing the bell," said Jones.

Voles, just about to pick up the cheque, paused.
He seemed to find himself at fault for a moment.
The jungle beast that hears the twig crack beneath

the foot of the man with the express rifle pauses like
that over his bloody meal on the carcase of the decoy
goat.

The door opened, and a servant appeared ; it was
the miracle with calves.

" Send out at once and bring in an officer—a policeman," said Jones.

" Yes, my lord."

The door shut.

Voles jumped up and seized his hat. Jones walked
to the door and locked it, placing the key in his
pocket.

" I've got you," said he, " and I'm going to squeeze
you, and I'm going to make you squeal."

" You're going to—you're going to—you're going
to—— " said Voles.

He was the colour of old ivory.

" I'm going to make you go through this——"

" Here ! D——n this nonsense ! Stop it, you fool !
I'll smash you ! " said Voles. " Here ! Open that
door and stop this business ! "

" I told you I was going to make you squeal," said
Jones ; " but that's nothing to what's coming."

Voles came to the table, and put down his hat.
Then, facing Jones, he rapped with the knuckles of his
right hand on the table.

" You've done it now," said he. " You've laid
yourself open to a nice charge, false imprisonment,
that's what you've done ! A nice thing in the papers
to-morrow morning, and intimidation on top of that.
Over and above those there's the papers. *I'll* have
no mercy. Those papers go to Lord Plinlimon to-
morrow morning, you'll be in the Divorce Court this
day month, and so will she. Reputation ! She won't
have a rag to cover herself with."

" Oh, won't she ? " said Jones. " This is most interesting."

He felt a great uplift of the heart. So this blackmail business had to do with a woman. The idea that Rochester was some horrible form of criminal had weighed upon him. It had seemed to him that no man would pay such a huge sum as eight thousand pounds in the way of blackmail unless his crime were in proportion. Rochester had evidently paid it to shield, not only his own name, but the name of a woman.

" Most interesting," said Voles. " I'm glad you think so ! " Then, in a burst : " Come, open that door, and stop this nonsense ! Take that key out of your pocket and open the door. You always were a fool, but this is beyond folly. The pair of you are in the hollow of my hand ! You know it. I can crush you like that—like that—like that ! "

He opened and shut his right hand. A cruel hand it was, hairy as to the back, huge as to the thumb.

Jones looked at him.

" You are wasting a lot of muscular energy," said he. " My determination is made, and it holds. You are going to prison, Mr. Filthy Beast Voles. I'm up against you, that's the plain truth. I'm going to cut you open, and show your inside to the British public. They'll be so lost in admiration at the sight, they won't bother about the woman or me. They'll call us public benefactors, I reckon. You know men, and you know when a man is determined. Look at me, look at me in the face, you sumph——"

A knock came at the door.

Jones took the key from his pocket and opened the door.

" The constable is here, my lord," said the servant.

" Tell him to come in," said Jones.

Voles had taken up his hat again, and he stood now by the table, hat in hand, looking exactly what he was, a criminal on his defence.

The constable was a fresh-looking and upstanding young man ; he had removed his helmet, and was carrying it by the chin-strap. He had no bludgeon, no revolver, yet he impressed Jones almost as much as he impressed the other.

" Officer," said Jones, " I have called you in for the purpose of giving this man in charge for attempt-ing—— "

" Stop ! " cried Voles.

Then something Oriental in his nature took charge of him. He rushed forward with arms out as though to embrace the policeman.

" It is all a mistake ! " cried he. " Constable, one moment, go outside one moment ! Leave me with his lordship. I will explain. There is nothing wrong, it is all a big mistake ! "

The constable held him off, glancing for orders at Jones.

Jones felt no vindictiveness towards Voles now ; disgust, such as he might have felt towards a vulture or a cormorant, but no vindictiveness.

He wanted that eight thousand pounds.

He had determined to make good in his new position, to fight the world that Rochester had failed to fight, and overcome the difficulties sure to be ahead of him. Voles was the first great difficulty, and, lo, it seemed that he was about not only to destroy it, but turn it to a profit. He did not want the eight thousand for himself ; he wanted it for the game, and the fascina-tion of that great game he was only just beginning to understand.

" Go outside, officer," said he to the constable.

He shut the door. " Sit down and write," said he.

Voles said not a word. He went to the table, sat down, and picked up the pen. The cheque was still lying there. He drew it towards him. Then he flung the pen down, then he picked it up, but he did not write. He waved it between finger and thumb, as though he were beating time to a miniature orchestra staged on the table before him. Then he began to write.

He was making out a cheque to the Earl of Rochester for the sum of eight thousand pounds, no shillings, no pence.

He signed it " A. S. Voles."

He was about to cross it, but Jones stopped him.

" Leave it open," said he. " And now one thing more. I must have those papers to-morrow morning without fail. And to make certain of them you must do this."

He went to the bureau and took a sheet of note-paper, which he laid before the other.

" Write," said he. " I will dictate. Begin ' June 2nd.' "

Voles put the date.

" ' My lord,' " went on the dictator, " ' this is to promise you that to-morrow morning I will hand to the messenger you send to me all the papers of yours in my possession. I confess to having held those papers over you for the purpose of blackmail, and of having obtained from you the sum of eight thousand pounds. And I promise to amend my ways and to endeavour to lead an honest life.

" (Signed) A. S. Voles.

" ' To the Earl of Rochester.' "

That was the letter.

Three times the rogue at the table refused to go on writing, and three times his master went to the door, the rattle of the door-handle always inspiring the scribe to renewed energy.

When the thing was finished, Jones read it over, blotted it, and put it in his pocket with the cheque.

"Now you can go," said he. "I will send a man to-morrow morning at eight o'clock to your home for the papers. I will not use this letter against you unless you give trouble. Well, what do you want?"

"Brandy!" gasped Voles. "For God's sake some brandy!"

CHAPTER IV

MORE INTRUDERS

THE little glass that had held the fin champagne stood on the table, the door was shut, Voles was gone, and the incident ended.

Jones, for the first time in his life, felt the faintness that comes after supreme exertion. He could never have imagined that a thing like that would have so upset him. He was unconscious during the whole of the business that he was putting out more energy than ordinary ; he knew it now as he contemplated the magnitude of his victory, sitting exhausted in the big, saddle-bag chair on the left of the fireplace and facing the door.

He had crushed the greatest rogue in London, taken from him eight thousand pounds of ill-gotten money, and freed himself of an incubus that would have made his position untenable.

Rochester could have done just the same, had he possessed daring and energy and courage enough. He hadn't, and there was an end of it.

At this moment a knock came to the door, and a flunkey—a new one—appeared.

" Dinner is served, my lord."

Jones sat up in his chair.

" Dinner ? " said he. "⁚ I'm not ready for it yet. Fetch me a whisky-and-soda ! Look here, tell Church I want to see him."

" Yes, my lord."

Jones possessed that very rare attribute—an eye for men. It was quite unknown to him ; up to this he had been condemned to take men as he found them, the pressure of circumstances alone had made him a business partner with Aaron Stringer. He had never trusted Stringer. Now, being in a position of command, he began to use this precious gift, and he selected Church for a first officer. He wanted a hench-man.

The whisky-and-soda arrived, and, almost imme-diately on it, Church.

Jones, placing the half-empty glass on the table, nodded to him.

" Come in," said he, " and shut the door."

Church closed the door and stood at attention. This admirable man's face was constructed not with a view to the easy interpretation of emotions. I doubt if an earthquake in Carlton House Terrace and the vicinity could have altered the expression of it.

He stood as if listening. Jones began :

" I want you to go to-morrow at eight o'clock to No. 12b, Jermyn Street, and get some documents for me. They will be handed to you by A. S. Voles."

" Yes, my lord."

" You will bring them back to me here."

" Yes, my lord."

" I have just seen the gentleman, and I've just dealt with him. He is a very great rogue, and I had to call an officer—a constable—in. I settled him."

Mr. Church opened his mouth as though he were going to speak. Then he shut it again.

" Go on," said Jones. " What were you going
to say ? "

" Well, your lordship, I was going to say that I
am very glad to hear that. When you told me, four
months ago, in confidence, what Voles was having out
of you, you will remember what advice I gave your
lordship. ' Don't be squeezed ! ' I said. ' Squeeze
him.' Your lordship's solicitor, Mr. Mortimer Collins,
I believe, told you the same."

" I have taken your advice. I find it so good, that
I am going to ask your advice often again. Do you
see any difference in me, Church ? "

" Yes, my lord, you have changed, if your lordship
will excuse me for saying so."

" How ? "

" You have grown younger, my lord, and more
yourself, and you speak different—sharper, so to say."

These words were balm of Gilead to Jones. He
had received no opinion of himself from others till now ;
he had vaguely mistrusted his voice, unable to estimate
in how much it differed from Rochester's. The
perfectly frank declaration of Church put his mind at
rest. He spoke sharper, that was all.

" Well," said he, " things are going to be different
all round—better, too."

He turned away towards the bureau, and Church
opened the door.

" You don't want me any longer, my lord ? "

" Not just now."

He opened Kelly's directory, and looked up the
solicitors till he came to the name he wanted.

Mortimer Collins, 10, Serjeants' Inn, Fleet Street.

" That's my man," said he to himself, " and to-
morrow I will see him." He opened the door and left
the room.

He did not know the position of the dining-room, nor did he want to. A servant seeing him, and taking it for granted that at this late hour he did not want to dress, opened a door.

Next minute he was seated alone at a large table, stared at by defunct Rochesters and their wives, and spreading his table napkin on his knees.

The dinner was excellent, though simple enough. English society has drifted a long way from the days when Lord Palmerston sat himself down to devour two helpings of turtle soup, the same of cod and oyster sauce, a huge plateful of York ham, a cut from the joint, a liberal supply of roast pheasant, to say nothing of kickshaws and sweets.

The days when the inside of a nobleman after dinner was a provision store, floating in sherry, hock, champagne, old port, and punch.

Nothing acts more quickly upon the nervous system than food. Before the roast chicken and salad were served, Jones found himself enjoying the dinner, and, more than that, enjoying his position.

The awful position of the morning had lost its terrors, the fog that had surrounded him was breaking. Wrecked on this strange, luxuriant, yet hostile coast, he had met the natives, fed with them, fought them, and measured their strength and cunning.

He was not afraid of them now. The members of the Senior Conservative Club camp had left him unimpressed, and the wild beast Voles had bequeathed to him a lively contempt for the mental powers of the man he had succeeded.

Rightly or wrongly, all lords caught a tinge of the lurid light that showed up Rochester's want of vim and mental hitting power.

But he did not feel a contempt for lords as such.

He was beginning to appreciate the fact that to be a lord was to be a very great thing. Even a lord who had let his estates run to ruin, like himself.

A single glass of champagne—he allowed himself only one—established this conviction in his mind, also the recognition that the flunkeys no longer oppressed him, they rather pleased him. They knew their work, and performed it perfectly, they hung on his every word and movement.

Yesterday, sitting where he was, he would have been feeling out of place and irritable and awkward ; even a few hours ago he would have felt oppressed and wanting to escape somewhere by himself. What lent him this new magic of assurance and sense of mastery of his position ? Undoubtedly it was his battle with Voles.

Coffee was served to him in the smoking-room, and there, sitting alone with a cigar, he began clearly, and for the first time, to envisage his plans for the future.

He could drop everything and run. Book a passage for the United States, enter New York as Lord Rochester, just as a diver enters the sea, and emerge as Jones. He could keep the eight thousand pounds with a clear conscience—or couldn't he ?

This point seemed a bit obscure.

He did not worry about it much. The main question had not to do with money. The main question was simply this : " Shall I be Victor Jones for the future, or shall I be the Earl of Rochester— the twenty-first Earl of Rochester ? Shall I clear out or stick to my guns ? Remain boss of this show, and try and make something of the wreckage, or sneak off with nothing to show for the most amazing experience man ever underwent ? "

Rochester had sneaked off. He was a quitter. Jones had once read a story in a popular magazine in which a railway manager had cast scorn on a ne'er-do-well.

"Heaven does surely hate a quitter," said the manager.

These words always remained with him. They had crystallized his sentiments in this respect ; the quitter ranked in his mind almost with the sharper.

All the same, the temptation to quit was strong, even though the temptation to stay was growing.

A loophole remained open to him. It was not necessary to decide at once ; he could throw down his cards at any moment and rise from the table if the game was getting too much for him, or if he grew tired of it.

He quite saw difficult times ahead for him in the mess in which Rochester had left his affairs—that was, perhaps, his strongest incentive to remain.

He was roused from his reverie by voices in the hall—loud, cheery voices.

A knock came to the door, and a servant announced :

" Sir Hugh Spicer and Captain Stark to see you, my lord."

Jones sat up in his chair.

" Show them in," said he.

The servant went out, and returned, ushering in a short, bibulous looking young man in evening dress, covered with a long, fawn-coloured overcoat ; this gentleman was followed by a half-bald, evil-looking man of fifty or so, also in evening attire.

This latter wore a monocle in what Jones afterwards mentally called " his twisted face."

" Look at him ! " cried the young man, " sitting in his blessed arm-chair and not dressed. Look at him ! "

5

He lurched slightly as he spoke, and brought up at the table, where he hit the inkstand with the cane he was carrying, sending inkpot and pens flying.

Jones looked at him.

This was Hughie. Pillar of the " Criterion " bar, president of the Rag Tag Club, baronet and detrimental —and all at twenty-three.

" Leave it alone, Hughie," said Stark, going to the silver cigar-box and helping himself. " Less of that blessed cane, Hughie—why, Jollops, what ails you ? "

' He stared at Jones as he lit a cigar. Jones looked at him.

This was Spencer Stark, late captain in His Majesty's Black Hussars, gambler, penniless, always well dressed, and always well fed—terrible. Just as beetles are beetles, whether dressed in tropical splendour or the funereal black of the English type, so are detrimentals detrimentals. Jones knew his men.

" I beg your pardon," said he. " Did you mean that name for me ? "

He rose as he spoke, and crossing to the bell, rang it. They thought he was speaking in jest and ringing for drinks ; they laughed, and Hughie began to yell, yell and slash the table with his cane in time to what he was yelling.

This beast, who was never happy unless smashing glasses, making a noise, or tormenting his neighbours, who had never been really sober for the space of some five years, who had destroyed a fine estate, and broken his mother's heart, seemed now endeavouring to break his wanghee cane on the table.

The noise was terrific.

The door opened and calves appeared.

" Throw that ruffian out," said Jones.

" Out with him ! " cried Hughie, throwing away

his cane at this joke. " Come on, Stark, let's shove old Jollops out of doors."

He advanced to the merry attack, and Stark, livened up by the other, closed in, receiving a blow on the midriff that seated him in the fender.

. The next moment Hughie found himself caught by a firm hand, that had somehow managed to insert itself between the back of his collar and his neck, gripping the collar.

Choking and crowing, he was rushed out of the room and across the hall to the front door, a running footman preceding him. The door was opened, and he was flung into the street.

The ejection of Stark was an easier matter. The hats and coats were flung out, and the door shut firmly.

" If either of those guys come here again," said Jones to the acolyte, " call an officer—I mean a constable."

" Yes, my lord."

" I wonder how many more people I will have to fling out of this house ? " said he to himself as he returned to the smoking-room. " My Heaven, what a mess that chap Rochester must have made all round ! Bar loungers like those ! Phew ! "

He ordered the ink to be cleared up, and then he sent for Mr. Church. He was excited.

" Church," said he, " I've shot out two more of that carrion. You know all the men I have been fool enough to know. If they come here again, tell the servants not to let them in."

But he had another object in sending for Church.

" Where's my cheque-book ? " he asked.

Church went to the bureau and opened a lower drawer.

" I think you placed it here, my lord." He produced it.

When he had gone Jones opened the book; it was one of Coutts's.

He knew his banker now as well as his solicitor. Then he sat down, and, taking Rochester's note from his pocket, began to study the handwriting and signature.

He made a hundred imitations of the signature, and found for the first time in his life that he was not bad at that sort of work.

Then he burnt the sheets of paper he had been using, put the cheque-book away, and looked at the clock. It pointed to eleven.

He switched out the lights and left the room, taking his way upstairs.

He felt sure of being able to find the bedroom he had left that morning, and coming along the softly-lit corridor he had no difficulty in locating it. He had half dreaded that the agile valet in the sleeved jacket might be there waiting to tuck him up, but, to his relief, the room was vacant.

He shut the door, and, going to the nearest window, pulled the blind up for a moment.

The moon was rising over London, and casting her light upon the Park. A huge summer moon. The sort of moon that conjures up ideas about guitars and balconies.

Jones undressed, and, putting on the silk pyjamas that were laid out for him, got into bed, leaving only the light burning by the bedside.

He tried to recall the details of that wonderful day, failed utterly, switched out the light, and went to sleep.

CHAPTER V

LADY PLINLIMON

THE most curious thing in the whole of Jones's extraordinary experiences was the way in which things affecting Rochester affected him.

The coldness of the club members was an instance in point. He knew that their coldness had nothing to do with him, yet he resented it practically just as much as though it had.

Then, again, the case of Voles. What had made him fight Voles with such vigour ? It did not matter to him in the least whether Voles gave Rochester away or not, yet he had fought Voles with all the feelings of the man who is attacked, not of the man who is defending another man from attack.

The attitude of Spicer and the other scamp had roused his ire on account of its want of respect for him, the supposed Earl of Rochester. Rochester's folly had inspired that want of respect, why should he (Jones) bother about it ? He did. It hit him just as much as though it were levelled against himself. He had found, as yet to a limited degree, but still he had found that anything that would hurt Rochester would hurt him, that his sensibility was just as acute under his new guise, and, wonder of wonders, his dignity as a lord just as sensitive as his dignity as a man.

If you had told Jones in Philadelphia that a day would come when he would be angry if a servant did not address him as " my lord," he would have thought you mad. Yet that day had come, or was coming, and that change in him was not in the least the result of snobbishness, it was the result of the knowledge of what was due to Rochester, Arthur Coningsby Delamere, twenty-first earl of, from whom he could not disentangle himself whilst acting his part.

He was awakened by Mr. Church pulling up his window blinds.

He had been dreaming of the boarding-house in Philadelphia where he used to live, of Miss Wybrow, the proprietress, and the other guests—Miss Sparrow, Mr. Moese (born Moses), Mr. Hoffman, the part-proprietor of Sharpes' Drug Store, Mrs. Bertine, and the rest.

He watched whilst Church passed to the door, received the morning tea-tray from the servant outside, and, placing it by the bed, withdrew. This was the only menial service which Church ever seemed to perform, with the exception of the stately carrying in of papers and letters at breakfast-time.

Jones drank his tea. Then he got up, went to the window, looked out at the sunlit Park, and then rang his bell. He was not depressed or nervous this morning. He felt extraordinarily fit. The powerful good spirits natural to him, a heritage better than a fortune, were his again. Life seemed wonderfully well worth living, and the game before him the only game worth playing.

Then the Mechanism came into the room and began to act. James was the name of this individual. Dumb and serious, and active as an insect, this man always filled Jones's mind with wonderment; he

seemed less a man than a machine. But at least he
was a perfect machine.

Fully dressed now, he was preparing to go down,
when a knock came to the door, and Church came in
with a big envelope on a salver.

" This is what you requested me to fetch from
Jermyn Street, my lord."

" Oh, you've been to Jermyn Street ? "

" Yes, my lord, directly I had served your tea, at
a quarter to eight I took a taxi."

" Good ! " said Jones.

He took the envelope, and Church and the
valet having withdrawn, he sat down by the
window to have a look at the contents.

The envelope contained letters.

Letters from a man to a woman. Letters from
the Earl of Rochester to Sapphira Plinlimon. The
most odiously and awfully stupid collection of love-
letters ever written by a fool to be read by a wigged
counsel in a divorce court.

They covered three months, and had been written
two years ago.

They were passionate, idealistic in parts, drivelling.
He called her his " Ickle teeny weeny treasure."
Baby language—Jones almost blushed as he read.

" He sure was moulting," said he as he dropped
letter after letter on the floor. " And he paid eight
thousand to hold these things back. Well, I don't
know, maybe I'd have done the same myself. I
can't fancy seeing myself in the *Philadelphia Ledger*
with this stuff tacked on to the end of my name."

He collected the incriminating documents, placed
them in the envelope, and came downstairs with it
in his hand.

Breakfast was an almost exact replica of the meal

of yesterday ; the pile of letters brought in by Church was rather smaller, however.

These letters were a new difficulty ; they would all have to be answered, the ones of yesterday and the ones of to-day.

He would have to secure the services of a typist and a typewriter ; that could be arranged later on. He placed them aside and opened a newspaper. He was accustomed enough now to his situation to be able to take an interest in the news of the day. At any moment his environment might split to admit of a new Voles or Spicer, or perhaps some more dangerous spectre engendered from the dubious past of Rochester. But he scarcely thought of this ; he had gone beyond fear, he was up to the neck in the business.

He glanced at the news of the day, reading as he ate. Then he pushed the paper aside. The thought had just occurred to him that Rochester had paid that eight thousand not to shield a woman's name but to shield his own ; to prevent that gibberish being read out against him in court.

This thought dimmed what had seemed a brighter side of Rochester, that obscure thing which Jones was condemned to unveil little by little and bit by bit. He pushed his plate away, and at this moment Church entered the breakfast-room.

He came to the table, and, speaking in a half-lowered voice, said :

" Lady Plinlimon to see you, your lordship."

" Lady Plinlimon ? "

" Yes, your lordship. I have shown her into the smoking-room."

Jones had finished breakfast. He rose from the table, gathered the letters together, and with them in his hand followed Church from the breakfast-room to the smoking-room. A· big woman in a big hat was seated in the arm-chair facing the door.

She was forty if an hour. She had a large, unpleasant face. A dominating face, fat-featured, selfish, and made up by art.

" Oh, here you are ! " said she as he entered and closed the door. " You see, I'm out early."

Jones nodded, went to the cigarette-box, took a cigarette, and lit it.

The woman got up and did likewise. She blew the cigarette-smoke through her nostrils, and Jones, as he watched, knew that he detested her. Then she sat down again. She seemed nervous.

" Is it true what I heard, that your sister has left you and gone to live with your mother ? "

" Yes," said Jones, remembering the bird-woman of yesterday morning.

" Well, you'll have some peace now, unless you let her back ; but I haven't come to talk of her. It's just this, I'm in a tight place."

" Oh ! "

" A very tight place. I've got to have some money ; I've got to have it to-day."

" Oh ! "

" Yes. I ought to have had it yesterday, but a deal I had on fell through. You've got to help me, Arthur."

" How much do you want ? "

" Fifteen hundred. I'll pay it back soon."

" Fifteen hundred pounds ? "

" Yes, of course."

A great white light, cold and clear as the dawn of truth, began to steal across the mind of Jones. Why had this woman come to him this morning so quickly after the defeat of Voles, who held her letters ? How

had Voles obtained those letters ?   This question had
occurred to him before, and this question seemed to
his practical mind pregnant now with possibilities.

" What do you want the money for ? " asked he.

" Good heavens ! What a question ! What does
a woman want money for ?   I want it, that's enough !
What else will you ask ? "

" What was the deal you expected money from
yesterday ? "

" A Stock Exchange business."

" What sort of business ? "

She crimsoned with anger.

" I haven't come to talk of that.   I came as a friend
to ask you for help. If you refuse—well, there that
ends it."

" Oh, no, it doesn't," said he.   " I want to ask you
a question."

" Well, ask it."

" It's just a simple question."

" Go on."

" You expected to receive fifteen hundred pounds
yesterday ? "

" I did."

" Did you expect to receive it from Mr. A. S. Voles ? "

He saw at once that she was guilty.   She half rose
from her chair, then she sat down again.

" What on earth do you mean ? " she cried.

" You know quite well what I mean," replied he.
" You would have had fifteen hundred of Voles' takings
on those letters. You heard last night I had refused
to part. He was only your agent. There's no use
in denying it. He told me all."

Her face had turned terrible, white as death, with
the rouge showing on the white.

" It is all untrue," she stuttered—" it is all untrue ! "

She rose, staggering. He 'did not want to pursue the painful business, the pursuit of a woman was not in his line. He went to the door and opened it for her.

" It is all untrue ! I'll write to you about this—untrue ! "

She uttered the words as she passed out. He reckoned she knew the way to the hall door, and, shutting the door of the room, he turned to the fireplace.

He was not elated. He was shocked. It seemed to him that he had never touched and handled wickedness before, and this was a woman in the highest ranks of life !

She had trapped Rochester into making love to her, and used Voles to extort eight thousand pounds from him on account of his letters.

She had hypnotized Rochester like a fowl. She was that sort. Held the divorce court over him as a threat. Could humanity descend lower ? He went to " Who's Who " and turned up the " P's " till he found the man he wanted.

" Plinlimon : Third baron, created 1831, Albert James, b. March 10th, 1862, o.s. of second baron and Julia, d. of J. H. Thompson, of Clifton, m.Sapphira, d. of Marcus Mulhausen ; educ. privately ; address, The Roost, Tite Street, Chelsea."

Thus spoke " Who's Who."

" I bet my bottom dollar that chap's been in it as well as she," said Jones, referring to Plinlimon, Albert James. Then a flash of humour lit the situation. Voles had returned eight thousand pounds ; as an agent he had received twenty-five per cent., say, therefore, he stood to lose at least six thousand. This pleased Jones more even than his victory He had a racial, radical, soul-rooted antipathy to Voles. Not an anger against him, just an antipathy. " Now," said he, as he placed " Who's Who " back on the bureau, " let's get off and see Mortimer Collins."

He left the house, and, calling a taxicab, ordered the driver to take him to Serjeants' Inn.   He had no plan of campaign as regards Collins.   He simply wanted to explore and find out about himself.   Knowledge to him in his extraordinary position was armour, and he wanted all the armour he could get, fighting, as he was, not only the living present, but also another man's past —and another man's character, or want of character.

CHAPTER VI

THE COAL-MINE

SERJEANTS' INN lies off Fleet Street, a quiet court, surrounded with houses given over to the law. The law has always lived there ever since that time when, as Stow quaintly put it, "There is in and about the City a whole university, as it were, of students, practisers, and pleaders, and judges of the laws of this realm, not living of common stipends, as in other universities it is for the most part done, but of their own private maintenance, as being fed either by their places or practices, or otherwise by their proper revenue, or exhibition of parents or friends— of their houses there be at this day fourteen in all, whereof nine do stand within the liberties of this City, and five in the suburbs thereof."

Serjeants' Inn stood within the liberties, and there to-day it still stands, dusty, sedate, once the abode of judges and serjeants, now the home of solicitors. On the right of entrance lay the offices of Mortimer Collins, an elderly man, quiet, subfusc in hue, tall, sparsely bearded, a collector of old prints in his spare hours, and one of the most respected members of his profession.

His practice lay chiefly amongst the nobility and landed gentry, a fact vaguely hinted at by the white or

yellow lettering on the tin deed-boxes that lined the
walls of his offices, setting forth such names and
statements as : " The Cave Estate," " Sir Jardine
Jardine," " The Blundell Estate," and so forth and
so on. He knew everyone, and everything about
everyone, and terrible things about some people, and
he was to be met with at the best houses. People
liked him for himself, and he inspired the trust that
comes from liking.

It was to this gentleman that Jones was shown in,
and it was by this gentleman that he was received—
coldly, it is true, but politely.

Jones, with his usual directness, began the business.

" I have come to have a serious talk with you,"
said he.

" Indeed ! " said the lawyer. " Has anything new
turned up ? "

" No ; I want to talk about my position generally.
I see that I have made a fool of myself."

The man of law raised his hands slightly with fingers
spread, the gesture was eloquent.

" But," went on the other, " I want to make good,
I want to clear up the mess."

The lawyer sighed. Then he took a small piece of
chamois leather from his waistcoat pocket and began
to polish his glasses.

" You remember what I told you the day before
yesterday," said he. " Have you determined to take
my advice ? Then you had nothing to offer me but
some wild talk about suicide."

" What advice ? "

Collins made an impatient gesture.

" Advice—why, to emigrate and try your luck in
the Colonies."

" H'm, h'm," said Jones. " Yes, I remember ; but

since then I have been thinking things out. I'm going to stay here and make good."

Again the lawyer made a gesture of impatience.

" You know your financial position as well as I do," said he. " How are you to make good, as you express it, against that position ? You can't ; you are hopelessly involved, held at every point. A month ago I told you to reduce your establishment and let Carlton House Terrace. You said you would, and you didn't. That hurt me. I would much sooner you had refused the suggestion. Well, the crash, if it does not come to-day, will come to-morrow. You are overdrawn at Coutts', you can raise money on nothing, your urgent debts to tradesmen and so forth amount, as you told me the day before yesterday, to over two thousand five hundred pounds. See for yourself how you stand."

" I say again," said Jones, " that I am going to make good. All these affairs seem to have gone to pieces because—I have been a fool."

" I'm glad you recognize that."

" But I'm a fool no longer. You know that business about Voles ? "

The man of affairs nodded.

" Well, what do you think of that ? " He took Voles' cheque from his pocket and laid it before the lawyer.

" Why, what is this ? " said the other. " Eight thousand pounds ! "

" He called on me for more blackmail," replied Jones, " and I squeezed him, called in a policeman, made him disgorge, and there's his cheque. Do you think he has money enough to meet it ? "

" Oh, yes, he is very wealthy ; but you told me *distinctly* he had only got a thousand out of you."

Jones swore mentally. To take up the life and past

of a rogue is bad, to take up the life and past of a weak-
kneed and shifty man is almost worse.

" I told you wrong," said he.

Collins suppressed a movement of irritation and
disgust.   He was used to dealing with humanity.

" What can a doctor do for a patient who holds
back essential facts ? " asked he.   " Nothing.   How
can I believe what you say ? "

" I don't know," replied the other.   " But I just ask
you to.   I ask you to believe I'm changed.   I've had a
shock that has altered my whole nature.   I'm not
the same man who talked to you the day before
yesterday."

Collins looked at him curiously.

" You have altered," said he, " your voice is different,
somehow, too.   I am not going to ask you *what* has
brought about this change in your views.   I can only
trust it may be so—and permanent."

" Bedrock," said Jones.   " I'm going to begin
right now.   I'm going to let that caravan——"

" Caravan ! "

" The Carlton House place.   Your idea is good ;
will you help me through with it ?   I don't know how
to start letting places ! "

" I will certainly assist you.   In fact, I believe I
can get you a tenant at once.   The Bracebridges want
just such a home, furnished.   I will get my clerk to
write to them—if you really mean it."

" I mean it."

" Well, that's something   I pressed the point about
your really meaning it because you were so violently
opposed to such a course when I spoke of it before.
In fact, you were almost personal, as though I had
proposed something disgraceful—though it was true
you came to agree with me at last."

" I guess the only disgrace is owing money and not being able to pay," said the present Lord Rochester. " I've come to see that."

" Thank Heaven ! " said Collins.

" I'll take rooms at a quiet hotel," went on the other ; " with this eight thousand and the rent from that gazabo, I ought to tide over the rocks."

" I don't see why not—I don't really see why not," replied Collins cheerfully, " if you are steadfast in your purpose. Fortunately, your wife's property is untouched, and now about her."

" Yes," said Jones, with a cold shiver.

" The love of a good wife," went on the other, " is a thing not to be bought ; and I may say I have very good reason to believe that, despite all that has occurred, you still have your wife's affection. Leaving everything else aside, I think your greatest mistake was having your sister to live with you. It does not do, and, considering Lady Venetia's peculiar temper, it especially did not do in your case. Now that things are different, would you care to see your wife and have a quiet talk over matters ? "

" No," said Jones hurriedly. " I don't want to see her—at least, not yet."

" Well, please yourself," replied the other. " Perhaps later on you will come to see things differently."

The conversation then closed, the lawyer promising to let him know should he secure an offer for the house.

Jones, so disturbed by his talk about his wife that he was revolving in his mind plans to cut the whole business, said good-bye, and took his departure. But he was not destined to leave the building just yet.

He was descending the narrow old stairs when he saw some people coming up, and drew back to let them pass.

6

A stout lady led the way, and was followed by an elderly gentleman and a younger lady in a large hat.

" Why it is Arthur ! " cried the stout woman. " How fortunate ! Arthur, we have come to see Mr. Collins. Such a terrible thing has happened."

The unfortunate Jones now perceived that the lady with the huge hat was the bird-woman, the elderly gentleman he had never seen before ; but the elderly gentleman had evidently often seen him—was most probably a near relative, to judge by the frigidity· and insolence of his nod and general demeanour. This old person had the Army stamp about him, and a very decided chin with a cleft in it.

" Better not talk out here," said he. " Come in— come in and see Collins."

Jones did not want in the least to go in and see Collins, but he was burning to know what this dreadful thing was that had happened. He half dreaded that it had to do with Rochester's suicide. He followed the party, and next moment found himself again in Collins' room, where the lawyer pointed out chairs to the ladies, closed the door, and came back to his desk-table, where he seated himself.

" Oh, Mr. Collins," said the elderly lady, " such a dreadful thing has happened ! Coal—they have found coal ! " She collapsed.

The old gentleman with the cleft chin took up the matter.

" This idiot," said he, indicating Jones, " has sold a coal-mine, worth maybe a million, for five thousand. The Glanafwyn property has turned up coal. I only heard of it last night, and by accident. Struthers said to me straight out in the club : ' Do you know that bit of land in Glamorgan Rochester sold to Marcus Mulhausen ? ' ' Yes,' I said. ' Well,' said he, ' it's not land, it's the top of the biggest coal-mine in Wales, steam coal, and Mulhausen is going to work it himself. He was offered two hundred and fifty thousand for the land last week ; they have been boring there for the last half year.' That's what he told me, and I verified it this morning. Of course, Mulhausen spotted the land for what it was worth, and laid his trap for this fool."

Jones restrained his emotions with an effort, not knowing in the least his relationship to the violent one. Mr. Collins made it clear.

" Your nephew has evidently fallen into a trap, your Grace," said he. Then, turning to Jones : " I warned you not to sell that land—Heaven knows, I knew little enough of the district and less of its mineral worth ; still, I was averse from parting with land—always am— and especially to such a sharp customer as Mulhausen. I told you to have an expert opinion. I had not minerals in my mind. I thought, possibly, it might be some railway extension in prospect—and it was your last bit of property without mortgage on it. Yes, I told you not to do it, and it's done."

" Oh, Arthur ! " sighed the elderly woman. " Your last bit of land ! And to think it should go like that ! I never dreamed I should have to say those words to my son." Then, stiffening and turning to Collins : " But I did not come to complain ; I came to see if justice cannot be done. This is robbery. That terrible man with the German name has robbed Arthur. It is quite plain. What can be done ? "

" Absolutely nothing ! " replied Collins.

" Nothing ? "

" Your ladyship must believe me when I say nothing can be done. What ground can we have for moving ? The sale was perfectly open and above board. Mulhausen made no false statements—I am right in saying that, am I not ? " turning to Jones.

Jones had to nod.

" And that being the case we are helpless."

" But if it can be proved that he knew there was coal in the land, and if he bought it concealing that knowledge, surely, surely the law can make him give it back," said the simple old lady, who, it would seem, was Rochester's unfortunate mother.

Mr. Collins almost smiled.

" Your ladyship, that would give no handle to the law. Now, for instance, if I know that the Canadian Pacific Railway, let us say, has discovered coal-bearing lands, and if I use that private knowledge to buy your Canadian Pacific stock, at, say, one hundred, and if that stock rose to three hundred, could you make me give you your stock back ? Certainly not. The gain would be a perfectly legitimate product of my own sharpness."

" Sharpness," said the bird-woman, " that's just it. If Arthur had had even sense, to say nothing of sharpness, things would have been very different all round— all round."

She protruded her head from her boa and retracted it. Jones, furious, dumb, with his hands in his pockets and his back against the window, said nothing.

He never could have imagined that a baiting like this, over a matter with which he had nothing to do, could have made him feel such a fool and such an ass.

He saw at once how Rochester had been done, and he felt, against all reason, the shame that Rochester might have felt, but probably wouldn't. His uncle, the Duke of Melford—for that was the choleric one's name—his mother, the dowager Countess of Rochester, and his sister, Lady Venetia Birdbrook, now all rose up and got together in a covey before making their exit and leaving this bad business and the fool who had brought it about.

You can fancy their feelings. A man in Rochester's position may be anything, almost, as long as he is wealthy, but should he add the crime of poverty to his other sins he is lost indeed. And Rochester had not only flung his money away, he had flung a coal-mine after it.

No wonder that his uncle did not even glance at him again as he left the room, shepherding the two women before him.

" It's unfortunate," said Collins, when they found themselves alone.

It was the mildest thing he could say, and he said it.

CHAPTER VII

THE GIRL IN THE VICTORIA

WHEN Jones found himself outside the office at last, and in the bustle of Fleet Street, he turned his steps westwards.

He had almost forgotten the half-formed determination to throw down his cards and get up from this strange game which he had formed when Collins had asked him whether he would not have an interview with his wife. This coal-mine business pushed everything else aside for the moment ; the thought of that deal galvanized the whole business side of his nature, so that, as he would have said himself, bristles stood on it. A mine worth a million pounds traded away for twenty-five thousand dollars !

He was taking the thing to heart, as though he himself had been tricked by Mulhausen, and now as he walked a block in the traffic brought him back from his thoughts, and suddenly a most appalling sensation came upon him. For a moment he had lost his identity. For a moment he was neither Rochester nor Jones, but just a void between these two. For a moment he could not tell which he was. For a moment he was neither. That was the terrible part of the feeling. It was due to over-taxation of the brain in his extraordinary position, and to the intensive

86

manner in which he had been playing the part of Rochester. It lasted, perhaps, only a few seconds, for it is difficult to measure the duration of mental processes, and it passed as rapidly as it had come.

Seeing a bar, he entered it, and a small glass of brandy closed the incident and made him forget it. He asked the way to Coutts's Bank, which in 1692 was situated at the Three Crowns in the Strand, next door to the Globe Tavern, and which still holds the same position in the world of commerce, and nearly the same in the world of bricks and mortar.

He reached the door of the bank, and was about to enter, when something checked him. It was the thought that he would have to endorse the cheque with Rochester's signature.

He had copied it so often that he felt competent to make a fair imitation ; but he had begun life in a bank, and he knew the awful eye a bank has for a customer's signature. His signature—at least, Rochester's—must be well-known at Coutts's. It would never do to put himself under the microscope like that ; besides— and this thought only came to him now—it might be just as well to have his money in some place unknown to others. Collins, and all that terrible family, knew that he was banking at Coutts's ; events might arise when it would be necessary for him to be able to lay his hands on a secret store of money.

He had passed the National Provincial Bank in the Strand. The name sounded safe, and he determined to go there.

He reached the bank, sent his name in to the manager, and was at once admitted. The manager was a solid man, semi-bald, with side-whiskers, and an air of old English business respectability delightful in these new and pushing days. He received the phantom of the

Earl of Rochester with the respect due to their mutual positions.

Jones, between Coutts's and the National Provincial, had done a lot of thinking. He foresaw that, even if he were to give in a passable imitation of Rochester's signature, all cheques signed in future would have to tally with that signature. Now, a man's handwriting, though varying, has a personality of its own, and he very much doubted as to whether he would be able to keep up that personality under the microscopic gaze of the bank people.

He decided on a bold course. He would retain his own handwriting. It was improbable that the National Provincial had ever seen Rochester's autograph ; even if they had, it was not a criminal thing for a man to alter his style of writing. He endorsed the cheque " Rochester," gave a sample of his signature, and gave directions for a cheque-book to be sent to him at Carlton House Terrace, and took his departure.

He had changed Rochester's five-pound note before going to Collins, and he had the change in his pocket —four pounds, sixteen and sixpence—five pounds, less the price of a cigar at the tobacconists' where he had changed his note, the taxi to Serjeants' Inn, and the glass of liqueur brandy. He remembered that he still owed for his luncheon yesterday at the Senior Conservative, and he determined to go and pay for it, and then lunch at some restaurant. Never again would he have luncheon at that Conservative caravanserai, so he told himself.

With this purpose in mind, he was standing at a crossing near Southampton Street, when a voice sounded in his ear, and an arm took his.

" Hello, Rochy ! " said the voice.

Jones turned, and found himself arm in arm with a youth of eighteen or so, a gilded youth, if ever there was a gilded youth, immaculately dressed, cheery, and with a frank face that was entirely pleasing.

" Hello ! " said Jones.

" What became of you that night ? " asked the cheery one as they crossed the road, still arm in arm.

" Which night ? "

" Which night ? Why, the night they shot us out of the Rag Tag Club. Are you asleep, Rawjester, or what ails you ? "

" Oh, I remember ! " said Jones.

They had unlinked now, and, walking along together, they passed through Trafalgar Square, the unknown doing all the talking, a task for which he seemed well qualified.

He talked of things, events, and people absolutely unknown to his listener, of horses and men and women. He talked Jones into Bond Street, and Jones went shopping with him, assisting him in the choice of two dozen coloured socks at Beale & Inman's. Outside the hosiers' the unknown was proposing luncheon, when a carriage, an open victoria, going slowly on account of the traffic, drew Jones's attention.

It was a very smart turn-out, one-horsed, but having two liveried servants on the box—a coachman and a footman with powdered hair.

In the victoria was seated one of the prettiest girls ever beheld by Jones, a lovely creature, dark, with deep, dreamy, vague, blue-grey eyes, and a face—ah, what pen could describe that face, so mobile, piquante, and filled with light and inexpressible charm !

She had caught Jones's eye ; she was gazing at him curiously, half mirthfully, half wrathfully, it seemed to him, and now, to his amazement, she made a little

movement of the head, as if to say " Come here."
At the same moment she spoke to the coachman.

" Portman, stop, please."

Jones advanced, raising his hat.

" I just want to tell you," said the beauty, leaning
a little forward, " that you are a silly old ass!
Venetia has told me all. It's nothing to me, but
don't do it. Portman, drive on."

" Good lord !" said Jones, as the vehicle passed
on its way, bearing off its beautiful occupant, of
whom nothing could now be seen but the lace-covered
back of a parasol.

He rejoined the unknown.

" Well," said the latter, " what has your wife been
saying to you ? "

" My *wife !* " said Jones.

" Well, your late wife, though you ain't divorced
yet, are you ? "

" No," said Jones.

He uttered the word mechanically, scarcely knowing
what he was saying.

That lovely creature his wife—Rochester's wife !

" Get in," said the unknown ; he had called a taxi.

Jones got in.

Rochester's wife ! The contrast between her and
Lady Plinlimon suddenly arose before him, together
with the folly of Rochester seen gigantically and in
a new light.

The taxi drew up in a street off Piccadilly ; they
got out, the unknown paid, and led the way into
a house whose front door presented a modest brass
doorplate inscribed with the words " Mr. Carr."

They passed along a passage, and then downstairs
to a large room, where small card-tables were set
out. An extraordinary room, for, occupying nearly

half of one side of it stood a kitchen range, over which a cook was engaged broiling chops and kidneys and all the other elements of a mixed grill. Old-fashioned pictures of sporting celebrities hung on the walls, and opposite the range stood a dresser laden with priceless old-fashioned crockery ware. Off this room lay the dining-room, and the whole place had an atmosphere of comfort and the days gone by when days were less laborious than our days, and comfort less allied to glitter and tinsel.

This was Carr's Club.

The unknown sat down before the visitors' book, and began to write his own name and the name of his guest.

Jones, looking over his shoulder, saw that his name was Spence—Patrick Spence. Sir Patrick Spence, for one of the attendants addressed him as Sir Patrick. A mixed grill, some cheese, and draught beer in heavy pewter tankards constituted the meal, during which the loquacious Spence kept up the conversation.

" I don't want to poke my nose into your affairs," said he, " but I can see there's something worrying you. You're not the same chap. Is it about the wife ? "

" No," said Jones, " it's not that."

" Well, I don't want to dig into your confidence, and I don't want to give you advice. If I did, I'd say make it up with her. You know very well, Rochy, you have led her the deuce of a dance. Your sister got me on about it the other night at the Vernons'. We had a long talk about you, Rochy, and we agreed you were the best of chaps, but too much given to gaiety and promiscuous larks. You should have heard me holding forth. But, joking apart, it's time you and I settled down, old chap. You can't

put old heads on young shoulders, but our shoulders
ain't so young as they used to be, Rochy. And I
want to tell you this, if you don't hitch up again in
harness the other party will do a bolt. I'm dead
serious. It's not the thing to say to another man,
but you and I haven't any secrets between us, and
we've always been pretty plain one to the other.
Well, this is what I want to say, and just take it as
it's meant. Maniloff is after her; you know that
chap, the attaché at the Russian Embassy, chap like
a billiard-marker, always at the other end of a cigarette
—other name's Boris. Hasn't a penny to bless himself with, I know he hasn't, for I've made kind inquiries
about him through Lewis. Reason why—he wanted
to buy one of my racers for export to Roosia. Seven
hundred down and the balance in six months. Lewis
served up his past to me on a charger. The chap's
rotten with debt, divorced from his wife, and a punter
at Monte Carlo. That's his real profession, and card
playing. He's a sleepy Slav, and if he was told his
house was on fire he'd say ' nichévo '—meaning it
don't matter, it's well insured. If he had a house to
insure, which he hasn't. But women like him, he's
that sort. But heaven help the woman that marries
him. He'd take her money and herself off to Monte,
and when he'd broken her heart and spoiled her life
and spent her coin he'd leave her and go off and be
Russian Attaché in Japan or somewhere. I know
him. Don't let her do it, Rochy."

" But how am I to help it ? " asked the perplexed
Jones, who saw the meaning of the other.

It did not matter in reality to him whether a woman
whom he had only seen once were to " bolt " with a
Russian and find ruination at Monte Carlo ; but this
world is not entirely a world of reality, and he felt a

surprisingly strong resentment at the idea of the girl in the victoria " bolting " with a Russian.

It will be remembered that in Collins's office the lawyer's talk about his " wife " had almost decided him to throw down his cards and quit.   This shadowy wife, first mentioned by the bird-woman, had, in fact, been the one vaguely felt insuperable obstacle in the way of his grand determination to make good where Rochester had failed, to fight Rochester's battles, to be the Earl of Rochester permanently, maybe, or, failing that, to retire and vanish back to the States with honourable pickings.

The sight of the real thing had, however, altered the whole position.   Romance had suddenly touched Victor Jones, the gorgeous but sordid veils through which he had been pushing had split to some mystic wand, and had become the foliage of fairyland.

" I want to tell you—you are an old ass ! "

Those words were surely enough to shatter any dream, to turn to bathos any situation.   In Jones's case they had acted as a most potent spell.   He could still hear the voice, wrathful, but with a tinge of mirth in it, golden, individual, entrancing.

" How are you to help it ? " said Spence.   " Why, go and make up with her again ; kick old Nichévo. Women like chaps that kick other chaps ; they pretend they don't, but they do.   Either do that, or take a gun and shoot her ; she'd be better shot than with that fellow."

He lit a cigarette, and they passed into the card-room, where Spence, looking at his watch, declared that he must be off to keep an appointment.   They said good-bye in the street, and Jones returned to Carlton House Terrace.

He had plenty to think about.

The pile of letters waiting to be answered on the table in the smoking-room reminded him that he had forgotten a most pressing necessity—a typist. He could sign letters all right, with a very good imitation of Rochester's signature, but a holograph letter in the same hand was beyond him. Then a bright idea came to him—why not answer these letters with a sixpenny telegram, which he could hand in himself ?

He found a sheaf of telegraph forms in the bureau, and sat down before the letters, dealing with them one by one, and as relevantly as he could. It was a rather interesting and amusing game, and when he had finished he felt fairly satisfied. " Awfully sorry can't come," was the reply to the dinner invitations. The letter signed " Childersley " worried him, till he looked up the name in " Who's Who," and found a lord answering to it at the same address as that on the note-paper.

He had struck by accident on one of the alleviations of a major misery of civilized life—replying to letters —and he felt like patenting it.

He left the house with the sheaf of telegrams, found the nearest post-office—which is situated directly opposite to Charing Cross Station—and returned. Then, lighting a cigar, he took the friendly and indefatigable " Who's Who " upon his knee, and began to turn the pages indolently. It is a most interesting volume for an idle moment, full of scattered romance, tales of struggle and adventure compressed into a few lines, peeps of history, and the epitaphs of still living men.

" I want to tell you—you are an old ass ! "

The words still sounding in his ears, made him turn again to the name Plinlimon. The contrast between Lady Plinlimon and the girl whose vision dominated his mind rose up again sharply at sight of the printed name.

Ass! That name did not apply to Rochester. To fit him with an appropriate pseudonym would be impossible. Fool, idiot, sumph—Jones tried them all on the image of the defunct, but they were too small.

" Plinlimon, 3rd Baron," read Jones, " created 1831. Albert James. B. March 10th, 1862. O.S. of second Baron and Julia, d. of J. H. Thompson, of Clifton ; m. Sapphira, d. of Marcus Mulhausen. Educ. privately. Address, the Roost, Tite Street, Chelsea."

Mulhausen! He almost dropped the book. Mulhausen! Collins, his office, and that terrible family party all rose up before him. Here was the scamp who had diddled Rochester out of the coal-mine, the father of the woman who had diddled him out of thousands. The paragraph in " Who's Who " turned from printed matter to a nest of wriggling vipers. He threw the book on the table, rose up, and began to pace the floor.

The girl-wife in the victoria, his own position— everything was forgotten before the monstrous fact half guessed, half seen.

Rochester had been plucked right and left by these harpies. He had received five thousand pounds for land worth a million from the father, he had paid eight thousand, or a good part of eight thousand, to the daughter. Fine business that !

I compared Jones, when he was fighting Voles, to a terrier. He had a good deal of the terrier in his composition, the honesty, the rooting-out instinct, and the fury before vermin. Men run in animal groups, and if you study animals you will be surprised by nothing so much as the old race fury that breaks out in the most civilized animal before the old race quarry or enemy.

For a few seconds, as he paced the floor, Jones was in the mental condition of a dog in proximity to a hutched badger. Then he began to think clearly. The obvious fact before him was that Voles, the Plinlimons, and Mulhausen were a gang ; the presumptive fact was that the money paid in blackmail had gone back to Mulhausen, or, at least, a great part of it.

Was Mulhausen the spider of the web ? Were all the rest his tools and implements ?

Jones had a good deal of instinctive knowledge of women. He did not in his heart believe that a woman could be so utterly vile as to use love letters directed to her for the purpose of extracting money from the man who wrote them. Or, rather, that, whilst she might use them, it was improbable that she would invent the method. The whole business had the stamp of a mind masculine and utterly unscrupulous. Even at first he had glimpsed this vaguely, when he considered it probable that Lord Plinlimon had a hand in the affair.

" Now," thought Jones, " if I could bring this home to Mulhausen, I could squeeze back that coal-mine from him. I could, sure."

He sat down and lit another cigar to assist him in dealing with this problem.

It was very easy to say " squeeze Mulhausen," it was a different thing to do it. He came to this conclusion after a few minutes' earnest concentration of mind on that problematical person. Hitherto he had been dealing with small men and wasters. Voles was a plain scoundrel, quite easily overthrown by direct methods. But Marcus Mulhausen he guessed to be a big man. The first thing to be done was to verify this supposition. He rang the bell and sent for Church.

" Come in," said he, when the latter appeared, " and shut the door. I want to ask you something."

" Yes, my lord."

" It's just this. I want you to tell me what you think of Lord Plinlimon, and what you have heard said about him ; I have my own opinions—I want yours."

" Well, my lord," began Church, " it's not for me to say anything against his lordship, but since you ask me, I will say that it's generally the opinion that his lordship is a bit—soft."

" Do you think he's straight ? "

" Yes, my lord—that is to say——"

" Spit it out," said Jones.

" Well, my lord, he owes money, that's well known ; and I've heard it said a good deal of money has been lost at cards in his house, but not through his fault. Indeed, you yourself said something to me to that effect, my lord."

" Yes, so I did ; but what I want to get at is this. Do you think he's a man who would do a scoundrelly thing—that's plain ? "

" Oh, no, my lord, he's straight enough. It's the other party."

" Meaning his wife ? "

" No, my lord—her brother, Mr. Julian."

" Ah ! "

Church warmed a bit.

" He's always about there—lives with them mostly. You see, my lord, he has no, what you may call, status of his own, but he manages to get known to people through her ladyship."

" Kind of sucker," said Jones.

Mr. Church assented. The expression was new to him, but it seemed to apply.

Then Jones dismissed him.

The light was becoming clearer and clearer. Here was another member of the gang, another instrument of Marcus Mulhausen.

" To-morrow," said Jones to himself, " I will go for these chaps. Voles is the key to the lot of them, and I have Voles completely under my thumb."

Then he put the matter from his mind for a while, and fell to thinking of the girl—his wife—Rochester's wife.

The strange thought came to him that she was a widow, and did not know it.

He dined out that night, going to a little restaurant in Soho, and he returned to bed early, so as to be fresh for the business of the morrow.

He had looked himself up again in " Who's Who," and found that his wife's name was Teresa. Teresa —the name pleased him vaguely, and now that he had captured it it stuck like a bur in his mind. If he could only make good over the Mulhausen proposition, recapture that mine, prove himself—would she, if he told her all—would she——

He fell asleep murmuring the word Teresa.

CHAPTER VIII

TERESA

H E woke up next morning to find the vision of Teresa, Countess of Rochester—so he called her—standing by his bedside.

Have you ever for a moment considered the influence of women ? Go to a public meeting composed entirely of men, and see what a heavy affair it can be—especially if you are a speaker ; sprinkle a few women through the audience, and behold the livening effect. At a party or a public meeting in the wheat pit or the battle-field, women, or the recollection of a woman, form or forms one of the greatest liveners to conversation, speech, or action. Most men fight the battle of life for a woman. Jones, as he sat up and drank his morning tea, gazing the while at the vision of Teresa, Countess of Rochester, had found, almost unknown to himself, a new incentive to action.

The position yesterday had begun to sag ; very little would have made him " quit," take a hundred pounds from the eight thousand, and a passage by the next boat to the States, but that girl in the victoria, those eyes, that voice, those words—they had altered everything.

Was he in love ? Perhaps not, but he was fascinated, held, dazzled.

More than that, the world seemed strange—brighter ; he felt younger, filled with an energy of a new brand. He whistled as he crossed the floor to look out of the window, and as he tubbed he splashed the water about like a boy.

It was easy to see that the unfortunate man had tumbled into a position more fantastic and infinitely more dangerous than any position he had hitherto occupied since setting foot in the house of Rochester.

That vanished and fantastic humorist would have found plenty to feed his thoughts could he have returned.

The cheque-book from the National Provincial Bank arrived by the first post, and after breakfast he put it aside in a drawer of the bureau in the smoking-room. He glanced through the usual sheaf of letters from unknown people, tradesmen whose accounts were marked "account rendered," and gentlemen who signed themselves with the names of towns and counties. One of the latter seemed indignant.

" I take this d——d bad of you, Rochester," said he. " I've found it out at last ; you are the man responsible for that telegram. I lost three days and a night's sleep rushing up to Cumberland on a wild-goose chase, and I'm telling people all about it. Some day you'll land yourself in a mess. Jokes that may be funny amongst Board school boys are out of place amongst men.—LANGWATHBY."

Jones determined to send Langwathby a telegram of apology when he had time to look his name up in " Who's Who," then he put the letters aside, called for his hat and cane, and left the house.

He was going to Voles first.

Voles was his big artillery. He guessed that the fight with Marcus Mulhausen would be a battle to the death. He reckoned a lot on Voles. In Trafalgar Square he called a taxi, and told the driver to take him to Jermyn Street.

PART III

CHAPTER I

THE ATTACK

A. S. VOLES, money-lender and bill discounter, lived over his business. That is to say his office was his dining-room. He owned the house in Jermyn Street. Jones, dismissing the taxi, rang the bell, and was admitted by a manservant, who, not sure whether Mr. Voles was in or not, invited the visitor into a small room on the right of the entrance-hall, and closed the door on him.

The room contained a desk-table, three chairs, a big-scale map of London, a Phœnix Insurance almanac, and a photogravure reproduction of Monna Lisa. The floor was covered with linoleum, and the window gave upon a blank wall.

This was the room where creditors and stray visitors had to wait. Jones took a chair and looked about him.

Humanity may be divided into three classes—those who, having seen, adore, those who tolerate, and those who detest Monna Lisa. Jones detested her. That leery, sleery, slippery, poisonous face was hateful to him as the mask of a serpent.

He was looking at the lady when the door opened, and in came Voles.

Voles looked yellower and older this morning, but his face showed nothing of resentment. The turning of the Earl of Rochester upon him had been the one great surprise of his life. He had always fancied that he knew character, and his fancy was not ill-founded. His confidence in himself had been shaken.

" Good morning, "said Jones. " I have come to have a little talk with you."

" Sit down," said Voles.

They seated themselves, Voles before the desk.

" I haven't come to fight," said Jones, " just to talk. You know that Marcus Mulhausen has got that Welsh land from me for five thousand, and that it is worth maybe a million now."

Voles nodded.

" Well, Mulhausen has to give that property back."

Voles laughed.

" You needn't laugh. You have seen my rough side. I'm holding the smooth towards you now—but there is no occasion to laugh. I'm going to skin Mulhausen."

" Well," said Voles, " what have I to do with that ? "

" You are the knife."

" Oh ! "

" Yes, indeed. Let's talk. When you got that eight thousand from me, you were only the agent of the Plinlimon woman, and she was only the agent of Marcus. She got something, you got something, but Marcus got the most ; Julian got something too, but it was Marcus got the joints. He gave you three the head, and the hoofs, and the innards, and the tail. I've had it out with the Plinlimon woman, and I know. You were a gang."

Voles heaved up in his chair.

" What more have you to say ? " asked he, thickly.

" A lot. There is nothing more difficult to get at than a gang, because they cover each other's traces. I pay you a certain sum in cash, you deduct your commission, and hand the remainder over to the Plinlimon woman ; she pays her father and gets a few hundred to pay her milliner. Who's to prove anything ? No cheques have passed."

" Just so," said Voles.

" I'm glad you see my point," replied Jones. " Now, if you can't untie a knot you can always cut it if you have a knife—can't you ? "

Voles shrugged his shoulders.

" Well, I said you were a knife, didn't I ? And I'm going to cut this knot with you. See my point ? "

" Not in the least."

" I'm sorry, because you make me speak plain, and that's unpleasant. This is my meaning. I have to get that property back, or else I will go to the police and rope in the whole gang. Tell the whole story. I will accuse Marcus. Do you understand that —Marcus and Marcus's daughter, and Marcus's son, and you ? And I won't do that to-morrow, I'll do it to-day. To-night the whole caboodle of you will be in gaol ! "

" You said you hadn't come to fight," cried Voles. " What do you want ? Haven't you had enough from me, yet you drive me like this ? It's dangerous."

" I have not come to fight. At least, not you. On the contrary, when I get this property back, if it turns out worth a million, I'll maybe pay you your losses. You've been paying the piper for Marcus, it seems to me."

" I have," groaned Voles.

The two words proved to Jones that he was right all through.

" Well, it's Marcus I'm up against, and you have to help me."

Then Voles began to speak. The something Oriental in his nature, the something that had driven him rushing with outspread arms at the constable that evening began now to talk.

Help against Marcus ! What could he do against Marcus ? Why, Marcus Mulhausen held him in the hollow of his hand—Marcus held everyone. His daughter, her husband, his own son, Julian, to say nothing of A. S. Voles and others.

Jones listened with patient attention to all this, and when the other had finished and wiped the palms of his hands on his handkerchief, said :

" But all the same, Marcus is held by the fact that he forms one of a gang."

Voles made a movement with his hand.

" Don't interrupt me. The head of a shark is the cleverest part of it, but it has to suffer with the body when the whole shark is caught. That's the fix Marcus is in. When I close on the lot of you, Marcus will be the first to go into the jug. Now, see here, you have got to take my orders ; they won't be hard."

" What are they ? "

" You have got to write me a note, which I will take to Marcus, telling him the game's up, the gang's burst, and to deliver."

" Why, d——n it, what ails you ? " said Voles.

" What ails me ? "

" You aren't talking like yourself—you have never been like yourself since you've taken this line."

Jones felt himself changing colour. In his excitement he had let his voice run away with him.

" It doesn't matter a button whether I'm like myself or not," said he ; " you've got to write that note, and do it now while I dictate."

Voles drummed on the desk with his fingers, then he took a sheet of paper and an envelope from a drawer.

" Well," said he, " what's it to be ? "

" Nothing alarming," said the other. " Just three words : ' It's all up.' How do you address him ? "

Without reply Voles wrote.

" Dear M.—It's all up."

" That'll do," said Jones. " Now sign your name and address the envelope."

Voles did so.

Jones put the letter in his pocket.

" Well," said he, " that ends the business. I hope with this, and what I have to say to him, Marcus will part, and, as I say, if things turn out as I hope, maybe I'll right your losses ; I have no quarrel with you— only Marcus."

Suddenly Voles spoke.

" For Heaven's sake," said he, " mind how you deal with that chap ; he's never been got the better of, curse him ; go cautiously ! "

" You never fear," said Jones.

CHAPTER II

JONES had already obtained Marcus Mulhausen's address from the invaluable " Kelly."

Mulhausen was a financier. A financier is a man who makes money without a trade or profession, and Mulhausen had made a great deal of money, despite this limitation, during his twenty years of business life, which had started humbly enough behind the counter of a pawnbroker's in the Minories.

His offices were situated in Chancery Lane. They consisted of three rooms, an outer waiting-room, a room inhabited by three clerks—that is to say, a senior clerk, Mr. Aaronson, and two subordinates—and an inner room where Mulhausen dwelt.

Jones, on giving his name, was shown at once into the inner room, where Mulhausen was seated at his desk.

Mulhausen was a man of sixty or so, small, fragile-looking, with grey side-whiskers and drowsy, heavy-lidded eyes.

He nodded to Jones, and indicated a chair. Then he finished his work, the reading of a letter, placed it under an agate paper-weight, and turned to the new-comer.

" What can I do for you this morning ? " asked Mulhausen.

" You can just read this letter," said Jones.

He handed over Voles' letter.

Mulhausen put on his glasses, opened the letter, and read it. Then he placed the open letter on top of the one beneath the agate paper-weight, tore up the envelope, and threw the two fragments into the waste-paper basket beside him.

" Anything more ? " asked he.

" Yes," replied the other, " a lot more. Let us begin at the beginning. You have obtained from me a piece of real estate worth anything up to a million pounds. You paid five thousand for it."

" Yes ! "

" You have got to hand me that property back."

" I beg your pardon," said Mulhausen. " Do you refer to the Glanafwyn lands ? "

" Yes."

" I see. And I have to hand those back to you—anything more ? "

" No, that's all. I received your daughter's letters back from Voles yesterday. Let's be plain with one another. Voles has confessed everything. I have his confession, under his own handwriting ; you are all in a net, the whole gang of you—you, your daughter, your son and Voles. You plucked me like a turkey. You know the whole affair as well as I do, and if I do not receive that property back before five o'clock to-day, I shall go to the nearest police office and swear an information against you."

" I see," said Mulhausen, without turning a hair, " you will put us all in prison, will you not ? That would be very unpleasant. Very unpleasant indeed."

He rose, went to some tin boxes situated on a ledge behind him, took out his keys and opened one.

Jones, fancying that he was going to produce the title-deeds, felt a little jump at his thyroid cartilage. This was victory without a battle. But Mr. Marcus Mulhausen took no title-deeds from the box. He produced a letter-case, came back with it to the table, and sat down.

Then, holding the letter-case before him, he looked at Jones over his glasses.

" You rogue," said Mulhausen.

That was the most terrific moment in Jones's life. Mulhausen from a criminal had suddenly become a judge. He spoke with such absolute conviction, ease, sense of power, and scorn that there could be no manner of doubt he held the winning cards. He opened the letter-case and produced a paper.

" Here is the bill of exchange for two hundred and fifty pounds to which you forged Sir Pleydell Tuffnell's name," said Marcus Mulhausen, spreading the paper before him. " That was two years ago. We all know Sir Pleydell and his easy-going ways. He is so careless you thought he would never find out, so good he would never prosecute. But it came into my hands, it is my property, and I have no hesitation in dealing with rogues. Now, do you suppose for a moment that if I were moving against you in any unlawful way —which I deny—I would have done so without a protector. Could you find a better protection than this ? The punishment for forgery, let me remind you, is five years' penal servitude at the least."

He looked down at the document with a cold smile, and then he glanced up again at his victim. Jones saw that he was done, done not by Marcus Mulhausen, but by Rochester. He had tripped over a kink in Rochester's character, just as a man trips over a kink in a carpet. Then rage came to him. The sight of the horrible scoundrel with whiskers, triumphant and gloating, roused the dog in his nature, and all the craft that lay hidden in him.

He heaved a sigh, rose brokenly, and approached the desk and the creature behind it.

" You are a cleverer man than I am," said he, " shake hands and call it quits."

Next moment he had snatched the paper from the fingers that held it, crumpled it, crammed it into his mouth. He rushed to the door and locked it, whilst Mulhausen, screaming like a woman, reached him and clutched him by the shoulders.

Then, swiftly turning, Jones gripped the financier by both arms, and held him so, chewing, chewing, chewing, mute and facing the shouting other one.

They were hammering at the door outside. Mr. Aaronson and the clerks, useless people for breaking-down-door purposes, were assisting their employer with their voices—mainly, the whole block of offices was raised, and boys and telephones were summoning the police.

Meanwhile, Jones was chewing, and the bill was slowly being converted into what the physiologist terms a bolus. It took three minutes before the bolus, properly salivated and raised by the tongue, passed the anterior pillars of the fauces, then the epiglottis shut down, and the bolus slipping over it, and seized by the muscles of the œsophagus, passed to its destined abode.

Jones had swallowed Rochester's past, or, at least, a most important part of it. The act accomplished, he sat down as a boa-constrictor recoils itself, still gulping. Marcus Mulhausen rushed to the door and opened it. A vast policeman stood before him, behind the policeman crowded Mr. Aaronson and the clerks, and behind these a dozen or two of the block dwellers, eager for gory sights at a distance.

Marcus looked round.

" What's all this ? " said he, " there is nothing wrong, just a little dispute with a gentleman.   It is all over.   Mr. Aaronson, clear the office.   Constable, here is two shillings for your trouble.   Good day."

He shut the door on the disappointed crowd, and turned to Jones.

The battle was over.

CHAPTER III

A WILD SURPRISE

A T five o'clock that day the transference of the property was made out and signed by Marcus Mulhausen in Mortimer Collins's office, and the Glanafwyn lands became again the property of the Earl of Rochester—"for the sum of five thousand pounds received and herewith acknowledged," said the document.

Needless to say, no five thousand pounds passed hands. Collins, mystified, asked no questions in the presence of Mulhausen. When the latter had taken his departure, however, he turned to Jones.

"Did you pay him five thousand?" asked the lawyer.

"Not a cent," replied the other.

"Well, how have you worked the miracle, then?"

Jones told.

"You see how I had them coopered," finished he. "Well, just as I was going to grab the kitty he played the ace of spades, produced an old document he held against me."

"Yes?"

"I pondered for a moment—then I came to a swift conclusion, took the doc. from him and ate it."

"You ate the document?"

" Sure."

Jones rubbed his stomach and laughed.

" Well, well," said the solicitor, with curious acquies-
cence and want of astonishment after the first momentary start caused by this surprising statement, " we
have the property back, that's the main thing."

" You remember," said Jones, " I talked to you
about letting that place ? "

" Carlton House Terrace ? "

" Yes ; well, that's off. I've made good. Do you
see ? "

" 'M—yes," replied Collins.

" I'll have enough money now to pay off the mort-
gages and things."

" Undoubtedly," said Collins. " But, now, don't
you think it would be a good thing if you were to tie
this property up, so that mischance can't touch it.
You have no children, it is true, but one never knows.
Honestly, I think you would be well advised if you were
to take precautions."

" Don't worry," said Jones brightly. " I'll give
the whole lot to my wife—when I can come to terms
with her."

" That's good hearing," replied the other.

Then Jones took his departure, leaving the precious
documents in the hands of the lawyer.

He was elated. He had proved the fact which he
had only guessed by instinct up to this, that a rogue
is the weakest person in the world before a plain dealer,
if the plain dealer has a weapon in his hand. The
almost instantaneous collapse of Voles and Mulhausen
was due to the fact that they stood on rotten founda-
tions. He told himself now, as he walked along home-
ward, that he need not have eaten that document.
Mulhausen would never have used it. If he had just

gone out and called in a policeman, Mulhausen, seeing him in earnest, would have collapsed.

However, the thing was eaten and done with, and there was no use in troubling any more on the matter. He had other things to think of. He had made good. He had saved the Rochester name and estates, he had recaptured one million eight thousand pounds, reckoning that the coal-bearing lands were worth a million, and, more than that, he was a sane man, able to look after what he had recaptured.

The Rochester family, if they knew, would have no cause to grumble at the interloper and the substitution of new brains and push in the place of decadence, craziness, and sloth. The day when he had changed places with Rochester was the best day that had ever dawned for them.

He was thinking this when, all of a sudden, that horrible, unreal feeling he had suffered from once before came upon him again. This time it was not a question of losing his identity, it was a shuffle of his over-taxed brain between two identities : Rochester—Jones— Jones—Rochester. It seemed to him, for the space of a couple of seconds, that he could not tell which of those two individuals he was ; then the feeling passed, and he resumed his way, reaching Carlton House Terrace shortly after six.

He gave his hat and cane and gloves to the flunkey who opened the door for him—he had obtained a latchkey from Church that morning, but forgot to use it—and was crossing the hall, when a strain of music brought him to a halt. The tones of a piano came from a door on the right. Someone was playing Chaminade's " Valse Tendre," and playing it to perfection.

Jones turned to the manservant.

" Who is that ? " he asked.

8

"It is her ladyship, my lord ; she arrived half an hour ago.   Her luggage has gone upstairs."

Her ladyship !

Jones, thrown off his balance, hesitated for a moment. *What* ladyship could it be ?   Not, surely, that awful mother !

He crossed to the door, opened it, found a music-room, and there, seated at a piano, the girl of the victoria.

She was in out-door dress, and had not removed her hat.

She looked over her shoulder at him as he came in ; her face wore a half-smile, but she did not stop playing. Anything more fascinating, more lovely, more distracting than that picture it would be hard to imagine.

As he crossed the room she suddenly ceased playing, and twirled round on the music-stool.

"I've come back," said she.   "Ju-Ju, I couldn't stand it.   You are bad, but you are a lot, lot better than your mother—and Venetia.   I'm going to try and put up with you a bit longer.   Ju-Ju, what makes you look so stiff and funny ? "

"I don't know," said Jones, passing his hand across his forehead.   "I've had a hard day."

She looked at him curiously for a moment, then pityingly, then kindly.

Then she jumped up, and made him sit down on a big couch by the wall, and took her seat beside him.

Then she took his hand.

"Ju-Ju, why will you be such a fool ? "

"I don't know," said Jones.

The caress of the little jewelled hand destroyed his mental powers.   He dared not look at her, just sat staring before him.

"They told me all about the coal-mine," she went

on, " at least, Venetia did, and how they all bully-ragged you—Venetia was great on that. Venetia waggled that awful gobbly-jick head of hers while she was telling me. They're *mad* over the loss of that coal thing. Oh, Ju-Ju, I'm so glad you lost it. It's wicked, I suppose, but I'm glad. That's what made me come back, the way they went on about you. I listened and listened, and then I broke out. I said all I've wanted to say for the last six months to Venetia. You know she told me how you came home the other night. I said nothing then, just listened and stored it up. Then, last night, when they all got together about the coal-mine, I went on listening and storing it up. Blunders was there as well as your mother and Venetia. Blunders said he had called you an ass, and that you were. Then I broke out. I said a whole lot of things—well, there it is. So I came back —there were other reasons as well. I don't want to be alone. I want to be cared for—I want to be cared for. When I saw you in Bond Street yesterday, I— I—I—— Ju-Ju, do you care for me ? "

" Yes," said Jones.

" I want to confess—I want to tell you something."

" Yes."

" If you didn't care for me—if I felt you didn't, I'd——"

" Yes."

" Kick over the traces, I would. I couldn't go on as I have been going, lonely, like a lost dog."

She raised his fingers and rubbed them along her lips.

" You will not be lonely," said the unfortunate man in a muted voice. " You need not be afraid of that."

The utter inadequacy of the remark came to him like one of those nightmare recognitions encountered as a rule only in dreamland. Yet she seemed to find it sufficient, her mind, perhaps, being engaged elsewhere.

" What would you have said if I had run away from you for good ? " asked she. " Would you have been sorry ? "

" Yes, dreadfully."

" Are you glad I've come back ? "

" I am."

" Honestly glad ? "

" Yes."

" Really glad ? "

" Yes."

" Truthfully, really, honestly glad ? "

" Yes."

" Well, so am I," said she. She released his hand.

" Now go and play me something. I want something soothing after Venetia—play me Chopin's ' Spianato '—we used to be fond of that."

Now, the only thing that Jones had ever played in his life was the " Star-Spangled Banner," and that with one finger—Chopin's " Spianato ! "

" No," he said. " I'd rather talk."

" Well, talk, then ! Mercy, there's the first gong ! "

A faint and far-away sound invaded the room, throbbed and ceased. She rose, picked up her gloves, which she had cast on a chair, and then peeped at herself in a mirror by the piano.

" You have never kissed me," said she, speaking as it were half to herself and half to him, seeming to be more engaged in a momentary piercing criticism of the hat she was wearing than in thoughts of kisses.

He came towards her like a schoolboy ; then, as she held up her face, he imprinted a chaste kiss upon her right cheek-bone.

Then the most delightful thing that ever happened to mortal man happened to him. Two warm palms suddenly took his face between them, and two moist lips met his own.

Then she was gone.

He took his seat on the music-stool, dazed, dazzled, delighted, shocked, frightened, triumphant !

The position was terrific.

Jones was no Lothario. He was a straight, plain, common-sensical man with a high respect for women, and the position of leading character in a bad French comedy was not for him. Jones would just as soon have thought of kissing another man's wife as of standing on his head in the middle of Broadway.

To personate another man, and to kiss the other man's wife under that disguise, would have seemed to him the meanest act any two-legged creature could perform.

And he had just done it. And the other man's wife had—hem ! His face still burned.

She had done it because of his deception.

He found himself suddenly face to face with the barrier that Fate had been cunningly constructing and had now placed straight before him.

There was no getting over it or under it ; he would have to declare his position *at once*—and what a position to declare !

She loved Rochester !

All at once that terrific fact appeared before him in its true proportions and its true meaning.

She loved Rochester.

He had to tell her the truth. Yet to tell her the truth he would have to tell her that the man she loved was dead.

Then she would want proofs.

He would have to bring up the Savoy Hotel people, fetch folk from America—disinter Rochester. Horror ! He had never thought of that. What had become of Rochester ? Up to this he had never thought once of what had become of the mortal remains of the defunct jester, nor had he cared a button—why should he ?

But the woman who loved Rochester would care. And he, Jones, would become in her eyes a ghoul, a monstrosity, a horror.

He felt a tinge of that feeling towards himself now. Up to this, Rochester had been for him a mechanical figure, an abstraction, but the fact of this woman's love had suddenly converted the abstraction into a human being.

He could not possibly tell her that he had left the remains of this human being, this man she loved, in the hands of unknown strangers—callously, as though it were the remains of an animal.

He could tell her nothing.

The game was up, he would have to quit. Either that, or to continue the masquerade, which was impossible, or tell her all, which was equally impossible.

Yet to quit would be to hit her cruelly. She loved Rochester !

Rochester, despite all his wickedness, frivolity, shiftlessness, and general unworthiness—or perhaps because of these things—had been able to make this woman love him, take his part against his family, and return to him.

To go away and leave her now would be the cruellest act. Cruel to her and just as cruel to himself, fascinated and held by her as he was. Yet there was no other course open to him. So he told himself—so he tried to tell himself, knowing full well that the only course open to him, as a man of honour, was a full confession of the facts of the case.

To sneak away would be the act of a coward, to impose himself on her as Rochester the act of a villain, to tell her the truth the act of a man.

The result would be terrific, yet only by facing that result could he come clear out of this business. For half an hour he sat, scarcely moving. He was up against that most insuperable obstacle, his own character. Had he been a crook, everything would have been easy ; being a fairly straight man everything was impossible.

He had got to this bed-rock fact when the door opened, and a servant made his appearance.

" Dinner is served, my lord."

Dinner !

He rose up and came into the hall. Standing there for a moment, undecided, he heard a laugh, and looked up. She was standing, in evening-dress, looking over the balustrade of the first landing.

" Why, you are not dressed ! " she said.

" I—I forgot," he answered.

Something fell at his feet—it was a rose. She had cast it to him, and now she was coming down the stairway towards him, where he stood, the rose in his hand and distraction at his heart.

" It is perfectly disgraceful of you," said she, looking him up and down and taking the rose from him, " and there is no time to dress now ; you usen't to be as careless as that." She put the rose in his coat. " I suppose it's from living alone for a fortnight with Venetia—what would a month have done ! "

She pressed the rose flat with her little palm.

Then she slipped her fingers through the crook of his elbow and led him to the breakfast-room door.

She entered and he followed her.

The breakfast-table had been reduced in size, and they dined facing one another across a bowl of blush roses.

That dinner was not a conversational success on the part of Jones, a fact which she scarcely perceived, being in high spirits and full of information she was eager to impart.

It did not seem to matter to her in the least whether the flunkeys in waiting were listening or not ; she talked of the family, of " your mater," and " Blunders " and " V.," and other people, touching, it seemed, on the most intimate matters, and all with lightness of tone and spirit that would have been delightful, no doubt, had he known the discussed ones more intimately, and had his mind been open to receive pleasurable impressions.

He would have to tell her directly after dinner the whole of his terrible story. It was as though Fate were saying to him, " You will have to kill her directly after dinner."

All that light-hearted chatter and new-found contentment, all that brightness would die. Grief for the man she loved, hatred of the man who had supplanted him, anguish, perplexity, terror would take their places.

When the terrible meal was over, she ordered coffee to be served in the music-room. He lingered behind for a moment, fiddling with a cigarette. Then, when he came into the hall, with the sweat standing in beads upon his forehead, he heard the notes of the piano.

It was a mazurka of Chopin's, played with gaiety and brilliancy, yet no funeral march ever sounded more fatefully in the ears of mortal.

He could not do it.

He could not possibly do it. No more than he could take one of those battle-axes wielded by defunct Rochesters, and, with it in his hand, go into the music-room and cut her down as she sat playing.

It was impossible.

He crossed to the music-room and opened the door.

CHAPTER IV

THE SECOND HONEYMOON

ONLY three of the electric lights were on in the music-room. In the rosy light and half shadows, the room looked larger than when seen in daylight and different.

She had wandered from the mazurka into Paderewski's Mélodie Op. 8, No. 3, a lonesome sort of tune it seemed to him, as he dropped into a chair, crossed his legs and listened.

Then, as he listened he began to think. Up to this his thoughts had been in confusion, chasing one another or pursued by the monstrosity of the situation. Now he was thinking clearly.

She was his, that girl sitting there at the piano with the light upon her hair, the light upon her bare shoulders and the sheeny fabric of her dress. He had only to stretch out his hand and take her. Absolutely his, and he had only met her twice. She was the most beautiful woman in London, she had a mind that would have made a plain woman attractive, and a manner delightful, full of surprises and contrarieties and tendernesses—and she loved him.

The "Arabian Nights" contained nothing like this, nor had the brain that conceived Tantalus risen to the heights achieved by accident and coincidence.

She finished the piece, rose, turned over some sheets of music, and then came across the room—floated across the room, and took her perch on the arm of the great chair in which he was sitting. Then he felt her fingers on his hair.

" I want to feel your bumps to see if you have improved—Ju-Ju ; your head isn't so flat as it used to be on top. It seems a different shape, somehow, nicer. Blunders is as flat as a pancake on top of his head. Flatness runs in families, I suppose. Look at Venetia's feet ! Ju-Ju, have you ever seen her in felt bath slippers ? "

" No."

" I have—and a long yellow dressing-gown, and her hair on her shoulders all wet, in rat tails. I'm not a cat, but she makes me feel like one, and talk like one. I want to forget her. Do you remember our honeymoon ? "

" Yes."

She had taken his hand and was holding it.

" We were happy then. Let's begin again, and let this be our second honeymoon, and we won't quarrel once—will we ? "

" No, we won't," said Jones.

She slipped down into the chair beside him, pulled his arm around her and held up her lips.

" Now, you're kissing me really," she murmured; " you seemed half frightened before—Ju-Ju, I want to make a confession."

" Yes ? "

" Well—somebody pretended to care for me very much a little while ago."

" Who was that ? "

" Never mind. I went the night before last to a dance at the Crawleys', and he was there."

" Yes."

" Yes—is that all you have to say ? You don't seem to be very much interested."

" I am, though."

" I don't want you to be too much interested, and go making scenes and all that—though you couldn't, for you don't know his name. Suffice to tell you— as the books say—he is a very handsome man, much, much handsomer than you, Ju.—Well, listen to me. He asked me to run off with him."

" Run off with him ? "

" Yes—to Spain. We were to go to Paris first, and then to Spain—Spain, at this time of year ! "

" What did you say ? "

" I said : ' Please don't be stupid.' I'd been reading a novel where a girl said that to a man who wanted to run off with her—she died at the end— but that's what she said at first. Fortunate I remembered it."

" Why ? "

" Because—because—for a moment I felt inclined to say ' yes.' I know it was dreadful, but think of my position, you going on like that, and me all alone with no one to care for me. It's like a crave for drink. I must have someone to care for me, and I thought you didn't—so I nearly said ' yes.' Once I had said what I did, I felt stronger."

" What did he say ? "

" He pleaded passionately—like the man in the book, and talked of roses and blue seas—he's not English—I sat thinking of Venetia in her felt bath- room slippers and yellow wrapper. You know she reads St. Thomas à Kempis and opens bazaars. She opened one the other day, and came back with her nose quite red and in a horrid temper—I wonder

what was inside that bazaar ? Well, I knew if I did
anything foolish Venetia would exult, and that held
me firm. She's not wicked. I believe she is really
good, as far as she knows how, and that's the terrible
thing about her. She goes to church twice on Sunday,
she takes puddings and things to old women in the
country, she opens bazaars and subscribes to ragged
schools—yet, with one word, she sets everyone by the
ears. Well, when I got home from the dance, I
began to think, and to-day, when they were all out,
I had my boxes packed, and came right back here.
I'd have given anything to see their faces when they
got home and found me gone."

She sprang up suddenly. A knock had come to
the door ; it opened and a servant announced Lady
Venetia Birdbrook.

Venetia had not changed that evening, she was
still in her big hat. She ignored Jones, and, standing,
spoke tersely to Teresa.

" So you have left us ? "

" Yes," replied the other. " I have come back
here, d'you mind ? "

" I ? " said Venetia. " It's not a question of my
minding in the least, only it was sudden, and as you
left no word as to where you were going, we thought
it best to make sure you were all right."

She took her seat uncomfortably on a chair, and the
Countess of Rochester perched herself again by Jones.

" Yes, I am all right," said she, with her hand
resting on his shoulder.

Venetia gulped.

" I am glad to know it," she said. " We tried to
make you comfortable. I cannot deny that mother
feels slightly hurt at having no word from you before
leaving, and one must admit that it cannot but seem

strange to the servants your going like that—but, of course, that is entirely a question of taste."

" You mean," said Teresa, " that it was bad taste on my part—well, I apologize. I am sorry, but the sudden craving to get—back here was more than I could resist. I would have written to-night."

" Oh, it does not matter," said Venetia, " the thing is done. Well, I must be going—but have you both thought over the future and all that it implies ? "

" Have we, Ju-Ju ? " asked the girl, caressingly stroking Jones's head.

" Yes," said Jones.

" I'm sure," went on Venetia with a sigh, " I have always done my best to keep things together. I failed. Was it my fault ? "

" No," said Teresa, aching for her to be gone. " I am sure it was not."

" I am glad to hear you say that. I always tried to avoid interfering in your life. I never did—or only when ordinary prudence made me speak, as, for instance, in that baccarat business."

" Don't rake up old things," said Teresa suddenly.

" And the Williamson affair," got in Venetia. " Oh, I am the very last to rake up things, as you call it. I, for one, will say no more of things that have happened, but I *must* speak on things that affect myself."

" What is affecting you ? "

" Just this. You know quite well the financial position. You know what the upkeep of this house means, you can't do it. You plainly can't do it. Your income is not sufficient."

" But how does that affect you ? "

" When tradespeople talk it affects me, it affects us all. Why not let this house and live quietly, some-where in the country, till things blow over ? "

" What do you mean by ' things blowing over ? ' "
asked Teresa. " One would think that you were
talking of some disgrace that had happened."

Venetia pulled up her long left-hand glove and
moved as though about to depart. She said nothing,
but looked at her glove.

During the whole of this time she had neither looked
at nor spoken to Jones, nor included him by word in
the conversation. Her influence had been working
upon him ever since she entered the room. He began
now more fully to understand the part she had played
in the life of Rochester. He felt that he wanted to talk
to Venetia as Rochester had, probably, never talked.

" A man once said to me that the greatest mistake
a fellow can make is to have a sister to live with him
after his marriage," said Jones.

Venetia pulled up her right-hand glove.

" A sister that has had to face mad intoxication,
and *worse*, can endorse that opinion," said she.

" What do you mean by ' worse ? ' " fired Teresa.

" I mean exactly what I say," replied Venetia.

" That is no answer. Do you mean that Arthur
has been unfaithful to me ? "

" I did not say that."

" Well, what can be worse than intoxication—that
is the only thing worse that I know of—unless murder.
Do you mean that he has murdered someone ? "

" I will not let you drag me into a quarrel," said
Venetia ; " you are putting things into my mouth. *I*
think mad extravagance is worse than intoxication,
inasmuch as it is committed by reasonable people
uninfluenced by drugs or alcohol. I think insults
levelled at inoffensive people are worse than the wildest
deeds committed under the influence of that demon,
alcohol."

" Who are the inoffensive people who have been insulted ? "

" Good gracious !—well, of course you don't know—you have not had to interview people."

" What people ? "

" Sir Joynson Harcourt, for instance, who had sixteen pianos sent to him only last week, to say nothing of pantechnicon vans and half the contents of Harrods' and Whiteley's, so that Arlington Street was blocked, simply blocked, the whole of last Friday."

" Did he say Arthur had sent them ? "

" He had no direct proof—but he knew.   There was no other man in London would have done such a thing."

" Did you send them, Ju-Ju ? "

" No," said Jones.   " I did not."

Venetia rose.

" You admitted to me, yourself, that you did," said she.

" I was only joking," he replied.

Teresa went to the bell and rang it.

" Good night," said Venetia, " after that I have nothing more to say."

" Thank goodness ! " murmured Teresa, when she was gone.   " She made me shiver with her talk about extravagance.   I've been horribly extravagant the last week—when a woman is distracted she runs to clothes for relief—anyhow, I did.   I've got three new evening frocks and I want to show you them.   I've never known your taste wrong."

" Good ! " said Jones.   " I'd like to see them."

" Guess what they cost ? "

" Can't."

" Two hundred and fifty—and they are a bargain. You're not shocked, are you ? "

" Not a bit."

" Well, come and look at them—what's the time ? Half-past ten." She led the way from the room and upstairs.

On the first landing she turned to the left, opened a door and disclosed a bedroom where a maid was moving about arranging things and unpacking boxes.

A large cardboard box lay open on the floor, it was filled with snow-white lingerie. The instinct to bolt came upon Jones so strongly that he might have obeyed it, only for the hand upon his arm pressing him down into a chair.

" Anne," said the Countess of Rochester, " bring out my new evening gowns, I want to show them."

Then she turned to the cardboard box. " Here's some more of my extravagance. I couldn't resist them. Venetia nearly had a fit when she saw the bill. Look ! "

She exhibited frilled and snow-white things, delicate and diaphanous and fit to be worn by angels. Then the dresses arrived, and were laid out on the bed and inspected. There was a black gown and a grey gown and a confection in pale blue. If Jones had been asked to price them he would have said a hundred dollars. Like most men he was absolutely unconscious of the worth of a woman's dress. To a woman, a Purdy and a ten-guinea Birmingham gun are just the same, and to a man, a ten-guinea Bayswater dress is little different, if worn by a pretty girl, from a seventy-guinea Bond Street—is it Bond Street ?— rig out. Unless he is a man-milliner.

Jones said " Beautiful ! " gave the palm to the blue, and watched them carried off again by the maid.

He had left his cigarettes downstairs, there were some in a box on a table, she made him take one and lit

9

it for him, then she disappeared into a room adjoining, returning in a few minutes dressed in a kimono covered with gold swallows and followed by the maid.   Then she took her seat before a great mirror, and the maid began to take down her hair and brush it.

As the brushing went on she talked to the maid and to Jones upon all sorts of subjects.   To the maid about the condition of her—Teresa's—hair, and a new fashion in hair-dressing ; to Jones about the Opera, the stoutness of Caruso, and kindred matters.

The hair having been arranged in one great, gorgeous plait, Jones, suddenly breaking free from a weird sort of hypnotism that had held him since first entering the room, rose to his feet.

" I'll be back in a minute," said he.

He crossed the room, reached the door, opened it and passed out, closing the door.   In the corridor he stood for half a moment with his hand to his head.

Then he came down the stairs, crossed the hall, seized a hat and overcoat, put them on and opened the hall door.

All the way down the stairs and across the hall, he felt as though he were being driven along by some viewless force, and now, standing at the door, that same force pushed him out of the house and on to the steps.

He closed the door, came down the steps, and turned to the right.

CHAPTER V

THE MENTAL TRAP

IT was a beautiful night, warm and starlit ; the waning moon had just begun to rise, and as he turned into St. James' Park a breath of tepid wind, grass-scented and balmy, blew in his face.

He walked in the direction of Buckingham Palace.

Where was he to go ? He had no ideas, no plans.

He had failed in performing the duty that Fate had arranged for him to perform. He had failed, but not through cowardice, or, at least, not through fear of consequences to himself.

The man who refuses to cut a lamb's throat, even though duty calls him to the act, has many things to be said for him.

His distracted mind was not dealing with this matter, however. What held him entirely was the thought of her waiting for him, and how she would feel when she found he had deserted her. He had acted like a brute, and she would hate him accordingly. Not him, but Rochester.

It was the same thing. The old story. Hatred, obloquy, disdain levelled against Rochester, affected him as though it were levelled against himself. He could not take refuge in his own personality. Even on the first day of his new life he had found that out at the club ; since then the struggle to maintain his position and the battles he had fought had steadily weakened his mental position as Jones, strengthened his position as Rochester.

The strange psychological fact was becoming plain, though not to him, that the jealousy he ought to have felt on account of this woman's love for Rochester was not there.

This woman had fascinated him, as woman had perhaps never fascinated a man before.   She had kissed him, she loved him, and though his reason told him quite plainly that he was Victor Jones, and that she loved and had kissed another man, his heart did not resent that fact.

Rochester was dead.   It seemed to him that Rochester had never lived.

He left the Park, and came along Knightsbridge, still thinking of her sitting there waiting for him, his mind straying from that to the kiss, the dinner, the bowl of roses that stood between them—her voice.

Then all at once these considerations vanished, all at once, and, like an extinguisher, fell on him that awful sensation of negation.

His mind, pulled this way and that between con-tending forces, became a blank written across with letters of fire, forming the question :

" Who am I ? "

The acutest physical suffering could not have been worse than that torture of the overtaxed brain, that feeling that if he did not clutch at *himself* he would become nothing.

He ran for a few yards, then it passed, and he found himself beneath a lamp-post, recovering and muttering his own name rapidly to himself, like a charm to exor-cise evil.

" Jones—Jones—Jones ! "

He looked around.

There were not many people to be seen, but a man and woman a few yards away were standing and looking at him. They had evidently stopped, and turned to see what he was about, and they went on when they saw him observing them.

They must have thought him mad.

The hot shame of the idea was a better stimulant than brandy. He walked on. He was no longer thinking of the woman before the mirror. He was thinking of himself.

He had been false to himself.

One of the greatest possessions any man can have in the world is himself. Some men let that priceless property depreciate, some improve it, it is given to few men to tamper with it after the fashion of Jones.

He saw this now, and, just as though a pit had opened before him, he drew back. He must stop this double life at once, and become his own self in reality ; failing to do that he would meet madness. He recognized this. No man's brain could stand what he had been going through for long. Had he been left to himself he might have adapted this mind gradually to the perpetual shifting from Jones to Rochester and vice versa. The woman had brought things to a crisis. The horror that had now suddenly fallen on him, the horror of the return of that awful feeling of negation, the horror of losing himself, cast all other considerations from his mind.

He must stop this business at once.

He would go away, return straight to America.

That was easy to be done—but would that save him ? Would that free him from this horrible, clinging personality that he had so lightly cast around himself ?

Nothing is stranger than mind. From the depth of his mind came the whisper "No." Intuition told him that were he to go to Timbuctoo, Rochester would cling to him, that he would wake up from sleep fancying himself Rochester, and then that feeling would return. What he required was the recognition by other people that he was himself (Jones), that the whole of this business was a deception, a stage play in real life. Their abuse, their threats, would not matter, their blows would be welcome, so he thought. Anything that would hit him back firmly into his real position in the scheme of things and save him from the dread of some day losing himself.

After a while the exercise and night air calmed his mind. He had come to the great decision. A decision immutable now, since it had to do with the very core of his being. He would tell her everything. To-morrow morning he could confess all. Her fascination upon him had loosened its hold, the terror had done that. He no longer loved her. Had he ever loved her? That was an open question, or, in other words, a question no man could answer. He only knew now that he did not crave for her regard, only for her recognition of himself as Jones.

She was the door out of the mental trap into which his mind had blundered.

These considerations had carried him far into a region of mean streets and suburban houses. It was long after twelve o'clock, and he fell to thinking what he should do with himself for the rest of the night. It was impossible to walk about till morning, and he determined to return to Carlton House Terrace, let himself in with his latch-key, and slip upstairs to his room. If by any chance she had not retired for the night, and he chanced to meet her on the stairs or in the hall, then the confession must be made forthwith.

It was after two o'clock when he reached the house. He opened the door with his key, and, closing it softly, crossed the hall and went up the stairs. One of the hall-lamps had been left burning, evidently for him ; a lamp was burning also in the corridor. He switched on the electric light in his room and closed the door.

Then he heaved a sigh of relief, undressed, and got into bed.

All across the hall, up the stairs, and along the corridor he had been followed by the dread of meeting her, and having to enter on that terrible explanation right away.

The craving to tell her all had been supplanted for the moment by the dread of the act.

In the morning it would be different. He would be rested and have command more over himself, so he fancied.

CHAPTER VI

ESCAPE CLOSED

HE was awakened by Mr. Church—one has always to give him the prefix—pulling up the blinds. His first thought was of the task before him.

The mind does a lot of quiet business of its own when the blinds are down and the body is asleep, and during the night his mind, working in the darkness, had cleared up matters, countered and cut off all sorts of fears and objections, and drawn up a definite plan.

He would tell her everything that morning. If she would not take his word for the facts, then he would have a meeting of the whole family. He felt absolutely certain that, explaining things bit by bit, and detail by detail, he could convince them of the death of Rochester and his own existence as Jones, absolutely certain that they would not push matters to the point of publicity. He held a trump card in the property he had recovered from Mulhausen, were he to be exposed publicly as an impostor all about the Plinlimon letters—Voles, and Mulhausen would come out; Mulhausen, that very astute practitioner, would not be long in declaring that he had been forced to return the title-deeds to protect his daughter's name; Voles would swear anything, and their case would stand good on the proved fact that he (Jones) was a swindler. No ; assuredly the family would not press the matter to publicity.

Having drunk his tea, he arose, bathed, and dressed with a calm mind.

Then he came downstairs.

She was not in the breakfast-room, where only one place was laid, and concluding that she was breakfasting in her own room, he sat down to table.

After the meal, and with another sheaf of the early post letters in his hand, he crossed to the smoking-room, where he closed the door, put the letters on the table, and lit a cigar. Then, having smoked for a few minutes and collected his thoughts, he rang the bell, and sent for Mr. Church.

" Church," said he, when that functionary arrived, " will you tell—my wife I want to see her ? "

" Her ladyship left last night, your lordship—she left at quarter to eleven."

" Left ! Where did she go to ? "

" She went to the South Kensington Hotel, your lordship."

" Good heavens, what made her—why did she go ? Ah, was it because I did not come back ? "

" I think it was, your lordship."

Mr. Church spoke gravely and the least bit stiffly. It could easily be seen that, as an old servant and faithful retainer, he was on the woman's side in the business.

" I had to go out," said the other. " I will explain it to her when I see her. It was on a matter of importance. Thanks, that will do, Church."

Alone again, he finished his cigar.

The awful fear of the night before, the fear of negation and the loss of himself, had vanished with a brain refreshed by sleep and before this fact.

What a brute he had been! She had come back forgiving him for who knows what; she had taken his part against his traducers, kissed him. She had fancied that all was right, and that happiness had returned, and he had coldly discarded her.

It would have been less cruel to have beaten her. She was a good, sweet woman. He knew that fact now, both instinctively and by knowledge. He had not recognized it fully till this minute.

Would it, after all, have been better to have deceived her, and to have played the part of Rochester? That question occurred to him for a moment, to be flung at once away. It was not only personal antagonism to such a course, nor the dread of madness owing to his double life, that cast it out so violently, but the recognition of the goodness and lovableness of the woman. Leaving everything else aside, to carry on such a deception with her, even to think of it, was impossible.

More than ever was he determined to clear this thing up and tell her all, and, to his honour be it said, his main motive now was to do his best by her.

He finished his cigar, and then going into the hall obtained his hat and left the house.

He did not know where the South Kensington Hotel might be, but a taxi solved that question, and shortly before ten o'clock he reached his destination.

Yes, Lady Rochester had arrived last night, and was staying in the hotel, and, whilst the girl in the manager's office was sending up his name and asking for an interview, Jones took his seat in the lounge.

A long time—nearly ten minutes—elapsed, and then a boy brought him her answer in the form of a letter.

He opened it.

" Never again.   This is good-bye.—T."

That was the answer.

He sat with the sheet of paper in his hand, con-templating the shape and make of an arm-chair of wicker-work opposite him.

What was he to do ?

He had just received the answer he might have expected, neither more nor less.   It was impossible for him to force an interview with her.   He had overthrown Voles, climbed over Mulhausen, but the flight of stairs dividing him now from the private suite of the Countess of Rochester was an obstacle not to be overcome by courage or direct methods, and he knew of no indirect methods.

He folded up the paper and put it in his pocket. Then he left the hotel and took his way back to Carlton House Terrace.

If she would not see him, she could not refuse to read a letter.   He would write to her and explain all.   He would write in detail, giving the whole business, circumstance by circumstance.   It would take him a long time, he guessed that, and ordinary paper would not do.   He had seen a stack of manu-script paper, however, in one of the drawers of the bureau, and having shut the door and lit a cigarette, he took some of the sheets of long foolscap, ruled thirty-four lines to the page, and sat down to the business.

This is what he said :

" LADY ROCHESTER,
           " I want you to read what follows carefully

and not to form an opinion on the matter till all the details are before you. This document is not a letter in the strict sense of the term, it's more in the nature of an invoice of the cargo of stupidity and bad luck which I, the writer—Victor Jones, of Philadelphia, have been freighted with by an all-wise Providence for its own incomprehensible ends."

Providence held him up for a moment. Was Providence neuter or masculine ? He risked it, and left it neuter, and continued.

When the servant announced luncheon, he had covered twenty sheets of paper, and had only arrived at the American bar of the " Savoy."

He went to luncheon, swallowed a whiting and half a cutlet, and returned.

He sat down, read what he had written, and tore it across.

That would never do. It was like the vast prelude to a begging letter. She would never read it through.

He started again, beginning this time in the American bar of the " Savoy," writing very carefully. He had reached, by tea-time, the reading of Rochester's death in the paper.

Well satisfied with his progress, he took afternoon tea, and then sat down comfortably to read what he had written.

He was aghast with the result. The things that had happened to him were believable because they had happened to him, but in cold writing they had an air of falsity. She would never believe this yarn. He tore the sheets across. Then he burned all he had written in the grate, took his seat in the arm-chair, and began to think of the devil.

Surely there was something diabolical in the whole

of this business and the manner in which everything and every circumstance headed him off from escape. After dinner he was sitting down to attempt a literary forlorn hope, when a sharp voice in the hall made him pause.

The door opened, and Venetia Birdbrook entered. She wore a new hat that seemed bigger than the one he had last beheld, and her manner was wild.

She shut the door, walked to the table, placed her parasol on it, and began peeling off a glove.

" She's gone," said Venetia.

Jones had risen to his feet.

" Who's gone ? "

" Teresa—gone with Maniloff."

He sat down. Then she blazed out.

" Are you going to do nothing ? Are you going to sit there and let us all be disgraced ? She's gone— she's going to Paris. It was through her maid I learned it. She's gone from the hotel by this—gone with Maniloff. Are you deaf or simply stupid ? You *must* follow her."

He rose.

" Follow her now, follow her and get her back ; there is just a chance. They are going to the ' Bristol.' The maid told everything. I will go with you. There is a train at nine o'clock from Victoria ; you have only just time to catch it."

" I have no money," said Jones, feeling in his pockets distractedly, " only about four pounds."

" I have," replied she, " and our car is at the door. Are you afraid, or is it that you don't mind ? "

" Come on ! " said Jones.

He rushed into the hall, seized a hat and overcoat and next minute was buried in a stuffy limousine with Venetia's sharp elbow poking him in the side.

He was furious.

There are people who seem born for the express purpose of setting other people by the ears. Venetia was one of them. Despite Voles, Mulhausen, debts, and want of balance, one might hazard the opinion that it was Venetia who had driven the unfortunate Rochester to his mad act.

The prospect of a journey to Paris with this woman in pursuit of another man's wife was bad enough, but it was not this prospect that made Jones furious, though assisting. No doubt it was Venetia herself.

She raised the devil in him, and on the journey to the station, though she said not a word, she managed to raise his exasperation with the world, herself, himself, and his vile position, to the limit just below the last. The last was to come.

At the station they walked through the crowd to the booking-office, where Venetia bought the tickets. Reminiscences of being taken on journeys as a small boy by his mother flitted across the mind of Jones, and did not improve his temper.

He looked at the clock. It wanted twenty minutes of the starting time, and he was in the act of evading a barrow of luggage when Venetia arrived with the tickets.

It had come into the mind of Jones that not only was he travelling to Paris with Lady Venetia Birdbrook, in pursuit of the wife of another man, but that they were travelling without luggage. If, in Philadelphia, he had dreamt of himself in such a position, he would have been disturbed as to the state of his health and the condition of his liver ; yet now, in reality, the thing did not seem preposterous. He was concerned as to the fact about the want of luggage.

" Look here," said he, " what are we to do ? I haven't even a suit of pyjamas. I haven't even a tooth-brush. No hotel will take us in ! "

" We don't want an hotel," said Venetia. " We'll come straight back if we can save Teresa. If not, if she insists in pursuing her mad course, you had better not come back at all. Come on, and let us take our places in the train."

They moved away, and she continued.

" For if she does you will never be able to hold up your head again. Everyone knows how you have behaved to her."

" Oh, stop it ! " said he irritably. " I have enough to think about ! "

" You ought to."

Only just those three words, yet they set him off.

" Ought I ? Well, what of yourself ? She told me last night things about *you*."

" About me ! What things ? "

" Never mind."

" But I do." She stopped and he stopped. " I mind very much. What things did she tell you ? "

" Nothing much, only that you worried the life out of her, and that though I was bad, you were worse."

Venetia sniffed. She was just turning to resume her way to the train when she stopped dead like a pointer.

" That's them," she said, in a hard, tense whisper.

Jones looked.

A veiled lady accompanied by a bearded man, with a folded umbrella under his arm, and following a porter laden with wraps and small luggage, were making their way through the crowd towards the train.

The veil did not hide her from him. He knew at once it was she.

It was then that Venetia's effect upon him acted as the contents of the white paper acts when emptied into the tumbler that holds the blue-paper half of the Seidlitz powder.

Venetia saw his face.

" Don't make a scene ! " she cried.

That was the stirring of the spoon.

He rushed up to the bearded man and caught him by the arm. The bearded one turned sharply and pushed him away. He was a big man, he looked a powerful man ; dressed up as a conquering hero he would have played the part to perfection—the sort of man women adore for their " power " and manliness. He had a cigarette between his thick, red, bearded lips.

Jones wasn't much to look at, but he had practised odd times at Joe Hennessy's, otherwise known as Ike Snidebaum, of Garden Street, Philadelphia, and he had the fighting pluck of a badger.

He struck out, missed, got a drum-sounder in on the ribs, right under the uplifted umbrella arm and the raised umbrella, and then, swift as light, got in an uppercut on the whiskers under the left side of the jaw.

The umbrella man sat down, as men sit when chairs are pulled from under them, shouting for help —that was the humorous and pitiable part of it— scrambled on to his feet, instantly to be downed again.

Then he lay on his back with arms out, pretending to be mortally injured.

The whole affair lasted only fifteen seconds.

You can fancy the scene.

Jones looked round. Venetia and the criminal,

having seen the display—and at the National Sporting Club you often pay five pounds to see worse—were moving away together through the throng, the floored one, with arms still out, was murmuring : " Brandee, brandee ! " into the ear of a kneeling porter, and a station policeman was at Jones's side.

Jones took him apart a few steps.

" I am the Earl of Rochester," said he, in a half whisper. " That guy has got what he wanted—never mind what he was doing. Kick the beast awake, and ask him if he wants to prosecute."

The constable came and stood over the head end of the sufferer, who was now leaning on one arm.

" Do you want to prosecute this gentleman ? " asked the constable.

" Nichévo," murmured the other, " no—no. Brandee ! "

" Thought so," said Jones.

Then he walked away towards the entrance with the constable.

" My address is Carlton House Terrace," said he. " When you get that chap on his pins you can tell him to come there and I'll give him another dose. Here's a sovereign for you."

" Thanks, your lordship," said the guardian of the peace. " You landed him fine, I will say. I didn't see the beginning of the scrap, but I saw the knock out. You won't have any more bother with him."

" I don't think so," said Jones.

He was elated, jubilant ; a weight seemed lifted from his mind, all his evil humour had vanished. The feel of those whiskers and the resisting jaw was still with him ; he had got one good blow in at circumstance and the world. He could have sung. He was coming out of the station when someone ran up from behind.

It was Venetia—Venetia, delirious and jabbering.

" Teresa is in the car ! You have done it now ! You have done it now ! What *made* you do this awful thing ? Are you mad ? Here in the open station, before everyone, you have h-h-heaped this last disgrace on us—on *me !* "

" Oh, shut up ! " said Jones.

He sighted the car, ran to it, and opened the door. A whimpering bundle in the corner stretched out hands as if to ward him off.

" Oh, oh, oh ! " sighed and murmured the bundle.

Jones caught one of the hands, leaned in, and kissed it. Then he turned to Venetia, who had followed him.

" Get in ! " he said.

She got in. He got in after her, and closed the door. Venetia put her head out of the window.

" Home ! " cried she to the chauffeur.

Jones said nothing till they had cleared the station precincts. Then he began to talk in the darkness, addressing his remarks to both women in a weird sort of monologue.

" All this is nothing," said he. " You must both forget it. When you hear what I have to tell you to-morrow you won't bother to remember all this. No one that counts saw that ; they were all strangers and making for the cars. I gave the officer a sovereign. What I have to say is this : I must have a meeting of the whole family to-morrow—to-morrow morning. Not about this affair—about something else, something entirely to do with me. I have been trying to explain all day—tried to write it out, but couldn't. I have to tell you something that will simply knock you all out of time."

Suddenly the sniffing bundle in the corner became articulate.

" I didn't want to do it ! I didn't want to do it ! I hate him ! Oh, Ju-Ju, if you had not treated me so last night I would never have done it ! Never, never, never ! "

" I know," he replied. " But it was not my fault leaving you like that. I had to go. You will know everything to-morrow. When you hear all you will very likely never speak to me again, though I am innocent enough, Lord knows."

Then came Venetia's voice :

" This is new. Heaven *knows* we have had disgrace enough ! What else is going to fall on us ? Why put it off till to-morrow ? What new thing have you done ? "

Before Jones could reply, the warm-hearted bundle in the corner ceased sniffing and turned on Venetia.

" No matter what he has done, you are his sister, and you have no right to accuse him ! "

" Accuse him ! " cried the outraged Venetia.

" Yes, accuse him. You don't say it, but you feel it. I believe you'd be glad in some wicked way if he had done anything really terrible."

Venetia made a noise like the sound emitted by a choking hen.

Teresa had put her finger on the spot.

Venetia was not a wicked woman. She was something nearly as bad—a righteous woman, one of the ever judges. The finding out of other people's sins gave her pleasure.

Before she could reply articulately, Jones interposed. An idea had suddenly entered his practical mind.

" Good Heavens ! " said he. " What has become of your luggage ? "

" I don't know and I don't care," replied the roused one. " Let it go with the rest."

The car drew up.

" You will stay with us to-night, I suppose ? " said Venetia coldly.

" I suppose so," replied the other.

Jones got out.

" I will call here to-morrow morning at nine o'clock," said he. " I want the whole family present." Then, to the unfortunate wife of the defunct Rochester : " Don't worry about what took place this evening. It was all my fault. You will think differently about me when you hear all in the morning."

She sighed and passed up the steps, following Venetia like a woman in a dream. When the door closed on them he took the number of the house, then at the street corner he looked at the name of the street. It was Curzon Street. Then he walked home.

Come what might, he had done a good evening's work. More than ever did he feel the charm of this woman, her loyalty, her power of honest love.

What a woman ! And what a fate !

It was at this moment, whilst walking home to Carlton House Terrace, that the true character of Rochester appeared before him in a new and lurid light.

Up to this Rochester had appeared to him mad, tricky, irresponsible ; but up to this he had not clearly seen the villainy of Rochester. The woman showed it. Rochester had picked up a stranger because of the mutual likeness, and sent him home to play his part, hoping, no doubt, to have a ghastly hit at his family. What about his wife ? He had either never thought of her or he had not cared.

And such a wife !

" That fellow ought to be dug up and cremated," said Jones to himself, as he opened the door with his latch-key. " He ought, sure. Well, I hope I'll cremate his reputation to-morrow."

Having smoked a cigar, he went upstairs and to bed.

He had been trying to think of how he would open the business on the morrow, of what he would say to start with. Then he gave up the attempt, determining to leave everything to the inspiration of the moment.

CHAPTER VII

THE FAMILY COUNCIL

HE arrived at Curzon Street at fifteen minutes after nine next morning, and was shown up to the drawing-room by the butler. Here he took his seat and waited the coming of the family, amusing himself as best he could by looking round at the furniture and pictures and listening to the sounds of the house and the street outside.

He heard taxi horns, the faint rumble of wheels, voices.

Now he heard someone running up the stairs outside—a servant probably, for the sound suddenly ceased, and was followed by a laugh, as though two servants had met on the stairs and were exchanging words.

One could not imagine any of that terrible family running up the stairs lightly or laughing. Then, after another minute or two, the door opened, and the Duke of Melford entered. He was in light tweeds with a buff waistcoat; he held a morning paper under his arm, and was polishing his eyeglasses.

He nodded at Jones.

"Morning," said his Grace, waddling to a chair and taking his seat. "The women will be up in a moment." He took his seat, and spread open the paper as if to

glance at the news. Then, looking over his spectacles :
" Glad to hear from Collins you've got that land back.
I was in there just after you left, and he told me."

" Yes," said Jones, " I've got it back."

He had no time to say more, as at that moment the
door opened and the " women " appeared, led by the
Dowager Countess of Rochester.

Venetia shut the door, and they took their seats
about the room ; whilst Jones, who had risen up,
reseated himself.

Then, with the deep breath of a man preparing for
a dive, he began :

" I have asked you all to come here this morning—
I asked you to meet me this morning because I just
want to tell you the truth. I am an intruder into
your family——"

" An intruder ? " cried the mother of the defunct.
" Arthur, what *are* you saying ? "

" One moment," went on he ; " I want to begin
by explaining what I have done for you all, and then,
perhaps, you will see that I am an honest man, even
though I am in a false position. In the last few days
I have got back one million and eight thousand
pounds—that is to say, the coal-mine property and
other money as well, one million and eight thousand
that would have been a dead loss only for me."

" You have acted like a man," said the Duke of
Melford. " Go on—what do you mean about intru-
sion ? "

" Let me tell the thing in my own way," said Jones
irritably. " The late Lord Rochester got dreadfully
involved owing to his own stupidity with a woman—
I call him the late Lord Rochester, because I have to
announce now the fact of his death."

The effect of this statement was surprising. The

four listeners sat like frozen corpses for a moment ; then they moved, casting terrified eyes at one another. It was the Duke of Melford who spoke.

" We will leave your father's name alone," said he. " Yes, we know he is dead—what more have you to say ? "

" I was not talking of my father," said Jones, beginning to get bogged and slightly confused, also angry ; " he was not my father. If you will only listen to me without interrupting, I will make things plain. I am talking of myself—or at least the man who I am representing, the Earl of Rochester. I say that I am not the Earl of Rochester, he is dead." He turned to Rochester's wife. " I *hate* to have to tell you this right out and in such a manner, but it has to be told. I am not your husband. I am an American. My name is Victor Jones, and I come from Philadelphia."

The Dowager Countess of Rochester, who had been leaning forward in her chair, sank back ; she had fainted.

Whilst Venetia and the Duke of Melford were bringing her to, the wife of Rochester, who had been staring at Jones in a terrified manner, ran from the room. She ran like a blind person with hands outspread.

Jones stood whilst the unfortunate lady was resuscitated. She returned to consciousness sobbing, and flipping her hands, and she was led from the room by Venetia. Beyond the door Jones heard her voice raised in lamentation :

" My boy—my poor boy ! "

Venetia had said nothing.

Jones had expected a scene, outcries, questions, but there was something in all this that was quite beyond him. They had asked no questions, seemed to take the whole thing for granted, Venetia especially.

The Duke of Melford shut the door.

" Your mother—I mean Lady Rochester's heart is not strong," said he, going to the bell and touching it. " I must send for the doctor to see her."

Jones, more than ever astonished by the coolness of the other, sat down again.

" Look here," said he, " I can't make you all out— you've called me no names—you haven't let me fully explain ; the old lady is the only one that seems to have taken the news in. Can't you understand what I have told you ? "

" Perfectly," said the old gentleman, " and it's the most extraordinary thing I have ever heard—and the most interesting. I want to have a long talk about it. James," to the servant who had answered the bell, " telephone for Dr. Cavendish. Her ladyship has had another attack."

" Dr. Cavendish has just been telephoned for, your Grace, and Dr. Simms."

" That will do," said his Grace. " Yes, 'pon my soul, it's quite extraordinary."

He took a cigar-case from his pocket, proffered a cigar, which Jones took, and then lit one himself.

" Look here ! " said Jones, suddenly alarmed by a new idea, " you aren't guying me, are you ? You haven't taken it into your heads that I've gone dotty— mad ? "

" Mad ! " cried the old gentleman, with a start. " Never—such an idea never entered my mind. Why—why should it ? "

" Only you take this thing so quietly."

" Quietly—well, what would you have ? My dear fellow, what is the good of shouting—ever ? Not a bit. It's bad form. I take everything as it comes."

" Well, then, listen whilst I tell you how all this

happened. I came over here some time ago to rope in a contract with the British Government over some steel fixtures. I was partner with a man named Aaron Stringer. Well, I failed on the contract, and found myself broke with less than ten pounds in my pocket. I was sitting in the ' Savoy ' lounge, when in came a man whom I knew at once by sight, but I couldn't place his name on him. We had drinks together in the American bar, then we went upstairs to the lounge. He would not tell me who he was. ' Look in the looking-glass behind you,' said he, ' and you will see who I am.' I looked and saw him. I was his twin image. I must tell you first that I had been having some champagne cocktails and a whisky-and-soda. I'm not used to drink ; we had a jamboree together, and dinner at some place, and then he sent me home as himself—I was blind.

" When I woke up next morning I said nothing, but lay low, thinking it was all a joke. I ought to have spoken at once, but didn't ; one makes mistakes in life——"

" We all do that," said the other. " Yes—go on."

" And later that day I opened a newspaper and saw my name, and that I had committed suicide. It was Rochester, of course, that had committed suicide ; did it on the Underground. Then I was in a nice fix. There I was in Rochester's clothes, with not a penny in my pockets ; couldn't go to the hotel, couldn't go anywhere—so I determined to be Rochester, for a while at least.

" I found his affairs in an awful muddle. You know that business about the coal-mine ? Well, I managed to right his affairs. I wasn't thinking of any profit to myself over the business—I just did it because it was the right thing to do.

" Now, I want to be perfectly plain with you. I might have carried on this game always, and lived in Rochester's shoes, only for two things : one is his wife, the other is a feeling that has been coming on me that if I carried on any longer I might go dotty. Times I've had attacks of a feeling that I did not know who I was. It's leading this double life, you know. Now I want to get right back and be myself, and cut clear of all this. You can't think what it has been, carrying on this double life, hearing the servants calling me ' your lordship.' I couldn't have imagined it would have acted on the brain so. I've been simply crazy to hear someone calling me by my right name. Well, that's the end of the matter. I want to settle up and get back to the States——"

The Duke listened attentively to all this.

Then he asked questions about America, scarcely seeming to follow the replies ; then the conversation, somehow, took a general turn, and at last the door opened and a servant appeared.

" Dr. Simms has arrived, your Grace."

The Duke of Melford rose from his chair.

" One moment," said he to Jones. He left the room, closing the door.

Jones tipped the ash off his cigar into a jardinière near by.

He was astonished and a bit disturbed by the cool manner in which his wonderful confession had been received.

" Can it be they are lying low and sending for the police ? " thought he.

He was debating this question, when the door opened and the duke walked in, followed by a bald, elderly, pleasant-looking man ; after this latter came a cadaverous gentleman, wearing glasses.

The bald man was Dr. Simms ; the cadaverous, Dr. Cavendish.

Simms nodded at Jones as though he knew him.

" I have asked these gentlemen, as friends of the family, to step in and talk about this matter before seeing Lady Rochester," said the duke. " She has been taken to her room, and is not yet prepared for visitors."

"I shall be delighted to help in any way," said Simms ; " my services, professional or private, are always at your disposal, your Grace." He sat down and turned to Jones. " Now tell us all about it," said he.

Cavendish took another chair, and the duke remained standing.

Jones felt irritated, felt somewhat as a maestro would feel who, having finished that musical obstacle race, the Grand Polonaise, finds himself requested to play it again.

" I've told the whole thing once," said he, " I can't go over it again. The duke knows."

Suddenly Cavendish spoke.

" I understand from what his Grace said on the stairs that there is some trouble about identity ? "

" Some trouble ? " said Jones. " I reckon you are right in calling it some trouble."

" You are Mr. Jones, I think ? " said Simms.

" Victor Jones was the name I was christened by," answered Jones.

" Quite so—American ? "

" American ! "

" Now, Mr. Jones, as a matter of formality, may I ask you where you live in America ? "

" Philadelphia."

" And in Philadelphia what might be your address ? "

" Number one thousand one hundred and one, Walnut Street," replied Jones.

Cavendish averted his head for a moment, and the duke shifted his position on the hearthrug, leaning his elbow on the mantel and caressing for a moment his chin.

Simms alone remained unmoved.

" Just so," said Simms. " Have you any family ? "

" Nope."

" I beg your pardon ? "

" No."

" I thought you said ' nope '—my mistake."

" Not a bit, I did say ' nope '—it's short for no."

" *Short* for no. I see, just so."

Cavendish interposed with an air of interest.

" How would you spell that word ? " asked he.

Jones resented Cavendish somehow.

" I don't know," said he ; " this isn't a spelling bee. N-o-p-e, I suspect. You gentlemen have undertaken to question me on behalf of the family as to my identity. I think we had better stick to that point."

" Just so," said Simms, " precisely——"

" Excuse me," said the Duke of Melford, " I think if Mr.—er—Jones wishes to prove his identity as Mr. Jones, he will admit that his actions will help. Now, Lord Rochester was a very, shall we say, fastidious person, quiet in his actions."

" Oh, was he ? " said Jones ; " that's news."

" Quiet, that is to say, in his movements ; let it stand at that. Now, my friend Collins said to me something about the eating of a document."

Jones bristled.

" Collins had no right to tell you that," said he. " I told him that privately. When did he tell you that ? "

" When I called, just after his interview with you.

He did not say it in any way offensively. In fact, he seemed to admire you for your energy and so forth."

" Did you, in fact, eat a document ? " asked Simms, with an air of bland interest.

" I did, and saved a very nasty situation, *and* a million of money."

" What was the document ? " asked Cavendish.

" A bill of exchange."

" Now, may I ask why you did that ? " queried Simms.

" No, you mayn't," replied Jones. " It's a private affair affecting the honour of another person."

" Quite so," said Simms. " But, just one more question. Did you hear a voice telling you to—er— eat this paper ? "

" Yes."

" What sort of voice was it ? "

" It was the sort of voice that belongs to common-sense."

" Ha, ha ! " laughed Cavendish. " Good, very good ! But there is just something I want to ask. How was it, Mr.—er—Jones, that you turned into your present form, exchanged your position, as it were, with the Earl of Rochester ? "

" Oh, lord ! " said Jones. Then to the Duke of Melford : " Tell them."

" Well," said the duke, " Mr. Jones was sitting in the lounge of an hotel when a gentleman entered whom he knew but could not recognize."

" Couldn't place his name," cut in Jones.

" Precisely. The gentleman said, ' Turn round and look in that mirror.' "

" You've left the drinks out," said Jones.

" True. Mr. Jones and the gentleman had partaken of certain drinks."

" What were the drinks ? " put in Simms.

" Champagne cocktails, whisky-and-soda, then a bottle of Bollinger—after," said Jones.

" Mr. Jones looked into the mirror," continued the duke, " and saw that he was the other gentleman— that is to say, Lord Rochester."

" No, the twin image," put in Jones.

" The twin image—well, after that more liquor was consumed."

" The chap doped me with drink, and sent me home as himself," cut in Jones. " And I woke up in a strange bed, with a guy pulling up the window-blinds."

" A guy ? " put in Cavendish.

" A chap. Church is his name. I thought I was being bamboozled, so I determined to play the part of Lord Rochester. You know the rest "—turning to the Duke of Melford.

" Well," said Cavendish, " I don't think we need ask any more questions of Mr. Jones. We are convinced, I believe, that Mr. Jones and—er—the Earl of Rochester are different ? "

" Quite so," said Simms. " We are sure of his *bona fides*, and, of course, it is for the family to decide how to meet this extraordinary situation. I am sure they will sympathize with Mr. Jones and make no trouble. It is quite evident he had no wrong intent."

" Now you are talking," said Jones.

" Quite so. One more question. Does it seem to you I have not been talking at all up to this ? "

Jones laughed.

" It seems to me you have uttered *one* word or two. Ask a bee in a bottle, has it been buzzing ? "

The cadaverous Cavendish, who, from his outward appearance presented no signs of a sense of humour, exploded at this hit ; but Simms remained unmoved.

" Quite so," said he. " Well, that's all that remains to be said. But, now as a professional man, has not all this tried you a good deal, Mr. Jones ? I should think it was enough to try any man's health."

" Oh, my health is all right," said Jones. " I can eat and all that, but times I've felt as if I wasn't one person or the other. That's one of my main reasons for quitting, leaving aside other things. You see, I had to carry on up to a certain point, and, if you'll excuse me blowing my own horn, I think I've not done bad. I could have put my claws on all that money. If I hadn't been a straight man, there's a lot of things I could have done, appears to me. Well, now that everything is settled, I think that ought to be taken into consideration. I don't ask much—just a commission on the money salved."

" Decidedly," said Simms. " In my opinion you are quite right. But as a professional man, my concern just a moment ago was about your health."

" Oh, the voyage back to the States will put that right."

" Quite so, but you will excuse my professional instinct—and I am giving you my services for nothing, if you will let me—I notice signs of nerve exhaustion. Let's look at your tongue."

Jones put out his tongue.

" Not bad," said Simms. " Now just cross your legs."

Jones crossed his legs right over left, and Simms, standing before him, gave him a little, sharp tap just under the right knee-cap. The leg flew out.

Jones laughed.

" Exaggerated patella reflex," said Simms. " Nerve fag, nothing more. A pill or two is all you want. You don't notice any difficulty in speech ? "

" Not much," said Jones, laughing.

" Say : 'Peter Piper picked a peck of pickled peppers.' "

" Peter Peter piped a pick——" began Jones, then he laughed.

" You can't say it," said Simms, cocking a wise eyebrow.

" You bet I can," said the patient. " Peter Piper pucked a pick——"

" Nerve exhaustion," said Simms.

" Say, doc," cut in Jones, beginning to feel slight alarm, " what are you getting at ? You're beginning to make me feel frightened. There's not anything really wrong with me, is there ? "

" Nothing but what can be righted by care," replied Simms.

" Let me try Mr. Jones with a lingual test," said Cavendish. " Say : ' She stood at the door of the fish-sauce shop in the Strand welcoming him in.' "

" She stood at the door of the fish-shauce shop in the Strand welcom-om-ming im," said Jones.

" H'm, h'm ! " said Cavendish.

" That's crazy," said Jones. " Nobody could say that. Oh, I'm all right. I reckon a little liver pill will fix me up."

The two doctors withdrew to a window and said a few words together. Then they both nodded to the Duke of Melford.

" Well," said the duke, " that's settled. And now, Mr. Jones, I hope you will stay here for luncheon."

Jones had had enough of that house.

" Thanks," said he, " but I think I'll be getting back. I want a walk. You'll find me at Carlton House Terrace, where we can finish up this business.

It's a weight off my mind, now everything is over. Whew! I can tell you, I'm hungry for the States."

He rose, and took his hat, which he had placed on the floor, nodded to the Duke of Melford, and turned to the door.

Simms was standing in front of the door.

" Excuse me," said Simms, " but I would not advise you to go out in your condition ; much better stay here till your nerves have recovered."

Jones stared at him.

" My nerves are all right," said he.

" Don't, my dear fellow," said Cavendish.

Jones turned and looked at him, then turned again to the door.

Simms was barring the way still.

" Don't talk nonsense," said Jones. " Think I was a baby. I tell you I'm all right. What on earth do you mean? Upon my soul, you're like a lot of children ! "

He tried to pass Simms.

" You must not leave this room yet," said Simms. " Pray quiet yourself."

" You mean to say you'll stop me ? "

" Yes."

Then in a flash he knew. These men had not been sent for to attend the Dowager Countess of Rochester ; they were alienists, and they considered him to be Rochester—Rochester gone mad.

Right from the first start of his confession he had been taken for a madman. That was why Venetia had said nothing ; that was why the old lady had fainted ; that was why his wife—at least Rochester's wife—had run from the room like a blind woman.

He stood appalled for a moment before this self-evident fact. Then he spoke :

" Open that door—get away from that door ! "

" Sit down and *quiet* yourself," said Simms, staring him full in the eye. " You—will—not—leave—this —house ! "

It was Simms who sat down, flung away by Jones.

Then Cavendish pinioned him from behind, the Duke of Melford shouted directions, Simms scrambled to his feet, and Jones, having won free of Cavendish, the rough-and-tumble began.

They fought all over the drawing-room, upsetting jardinières, little tables, costly china.

Jones's foot went into a china cabinet, carrying destruction amongst a concert party of little Dresden figures ; Simms' portly behind bumped against a pedestal bearing a portrait bust of the nineteenth Countess of Rochester, upsetting pedestal and smashing bust ; and the Duke of Melford, fine old sportsman that he was, assisting in the business with the activity of a boy of eighteen, received a kick on the shin that recalled Eton across a long vista of years.

Then at last they had him down on a sofa, his hands tied behind his back with the duke's bandanna handkerchief.

Jones uttered no cry, the others no sound, but the bumping and banging and smashing had been heard all over the house. A tap came to the door, and a voice. The duke rushed to the door and opened it.

" Nothing ! " said he. " Nothing wrong ! Off with you ! "

He shut the door and turned to the couch.

Jones caught a glimpse of himself in a big mirror, happily unsmashed—caught a glimpse of himself all tumbled and tousled, with Simms beside him, and Cavendish standing by, refixing his glasses.

He recognized a terrible fact. Though he had smashed hundreds of pounds' worth of property, though he had fought these men like a mad bull, now that the fight was over, they showed not the least sign of resentment. Simms was patting his shoulder.

He had become possessed of the mournful privilege of the insane, to fight without raising ire in one's antagonists, to smash with impunity, to murder, without being brought to justice.

Also he recognized that he had been a fool. He had acted like a madman—that is to say, like a man furious with anger. Anger and madness have awful similarities.

He moved slightly away from Simms.

" I reckon I've been a fool," said he. " Three to one is not fair play. Come, let my hands free. I won't fight any more."

" Certainly," said Simms. " But let me point out that we were not fighting you in the least, only preventing you from taking a course detrimental to your health. Cavendish, will you kindly untie that absurd handkerchief ? "

Cavendish obeyed, and Jones, his hands freed, rubbed his wrists.

" What are you going to do now ? " asked he.

" Nothing," said Simms. " You are perfectly free, but we don't want you to go out till your health is perfectly restored. I know you will say that you feel all right. No matter. Take a physician's advice and just remain here quiet for a little while. Shall we go to the library, where you can amuse yourself with the newspaper or a book whilst I make up a little prescription for you ? "

" Look here ! " said Jones. " Let's talk quietly for a moment. You think I'm mad ? "

" Not in the least," said Simms. " You are only suffering from a nerve upset."

" Well, if I'm not mad, you have no right to keep me here."

This was cunning, but, unfortunately, cunning, like anger, is an attribute of madness, as well as of sanity.

" Now," said Simms, with an air of great frankness, " do you think that it is for our pleasure that we ask you to stay here for a while ? We are not keeping you—just asking you to stay. We will go down to the library, and I will just have a prescription made up ; then, when you have considered matters a bit, you can use your own discretion about going."

Jones recognized at once that there was no use in trying to fight this man with any other weapon than subtlety. He was fairly trapped. His tale was such that no man would believe it, and, persisting in that tale, he would be held as a lunatic. On top of the tale was Rochester's bad reputation for sanity. They called him " mad Rochester."

Then, as he rose up and followed to the library, a last inspiration seized him.

He stopped at the drawing-room door.

" Look here," said he, " one moment. I can·prove what I say. You send out a man to Philadelphia and make inquiries, fetch some of the people over that knew me. You'll find I'm—myself, and that I've told you no lie."

" We will do anything you like," said Simms, " but first let us go down to the library."

They went. It was a large, pleasant room lined with books.

Simms sat down at the writing-table, whilst the others took chairs. He wrote a prescription, and the duke, ringing the bell, ordered a servant to take the prescription to the chemist's.

Then during the twenty minutes before the servant returned they talked. Jones, giving again his address, that fantastic address which was yet real, and the names and descriptions of people he knew and who would know him.

" You see, gentlemen," said he, " it's just this. I have only one crave in life just now—to be myself again. Not exactly that, but to be recognized as myself. You can't imagine what that feeling is. You needn't tell me. I know exactly what you think —you think I'm Rochester gone crazy. I know the yarn I've slung you sounds crazy, but it's the truth. The fact is I've felt at times that if I didn't get some-one to recognize me as myself, I'd *go* crazy. Just one person to believe in me ; that's all I want, and then I'd feel free of this cursed Rochester. Put yourself in my place. Imagine that you have lost touch with everything you ever were ; that you were playing another man's part, and that everyone in the world kept on insisting you were the other guy. Think of that for a position ! Why, gentlemen, you might open that door wide. I wouldn't want to go out, not till I had convinced one of you, at all events, that my story was true. I wouldn't want to go back to the States, not till I had convinced you that I am who I am. It seems foolish, but it's a bed-rock fact. I have to make good on this position—convince some-one who knows the facts, and so get myself back. It wouldn't be any use my going to Philadelphia. I'd say to people I know there, ' I'm Jones ' ; they'd say, ' Of course you are,' and believe me. But then, do you see, they wouldn't know of this adventure, and their belief in me wouldn't be a bit of good. Of course

I *know* I'm Jones ; all the same, I've been playing the part of Rochester so hard that times I've almost believed I'm him, times I've lost myself, and I have a feeling at the back of my mind that if I don't get someone to believe me to be who I am, I may go dotty in earnest. It's a feeling without reason, I know. It's more like having a grit in the eye than anything else. I want to get rid of that grit, and I can't take it out myself, someone else must do it. One person would be enough, just one person to believe in what I say, and I would be myself again. That's why I want you to send to Philadelphia. The mind is a curious thing, gentlemen ; the freedom of the body is nothing if the mind is not free, and my mind can never be free till another person, who knows my whole story, believes in what I say. I could not have imagined anyone being trapped like this ; I've heard of an actor guy once playing a part so often he went loony, and fancied himself the character. I'm not like that ; I'm as sane as you. It's just this uneasy, uncomfortable feeling—this want to get absolutely clean out of this business, that's the trouble."

" Never mind ! " said Simms cheerfully, " we will get you out, only you must *not* worry yourself. I admit that your story is strange, but we will send to Philadelphia and make all inquiries—come in."

The servant had knocked at the door. He entered with the medicine. Simms sent him for a wine-glass, and when it arrived he poured out a dose.

" Now take a dose of your medicine like a man," said the kindly physician, jocularly, " and another in four hours' time ; it will remake your nerves."

Jones tossed the stuff off impatiently.

" Say," said he, " there's another point I've forgot. You might go to the ' Savoy ' and get the clerk there, he'd recognize me ; the bar-tender in the American bar, he'd maybe be able to recognize me too ; he saw us together—I say, I feel a bit drowsy ; you haven't doped me, have you ? "

Simms and Cavendish, leaving the house together five minutes later, had a moment's conversation on the steps.

" What do you think of him ? " said Simms.

" Bad," said Cavendish. " He reasons on his own case, that's always bad ; and did you notice how cleverly he worked that in about wanting someone to believe in him ? "

They walked down the street together.

" That smash has been coming for a long time," said Simms—" it's an heirloom. It's a good thing it has come ; he was getting to be a by-word. I wonder what it is that introduces the humorous element into insanity ?—that address, for instance, a thousand one hundred and one, Walnut Street, could never have strayed into a sane person's head."

" Nor a luncheon on bills of exchange," said Cavendish. " Well, he will be all right at Hoover's. What was the dose you gave him ? "

" Heroin, mostly," replied the other. " Well, so long. I must send Trapson to see him now, on account of the certificate." Trapson was another alienist, the Law of England holding that a patient must be seen separately by two doctors before being interned in an asylum.

CHAPTER VIII

HOOVER'S

JONES, after the magic draught administered by Simms, entered into a blissful condition of twilight sleep—half sleep, half drowsiness, absolute indifference, broken by a vague vision of Trapson. He walked with assistance to the hall door, and entered a motor-car ; it did not matter to him what he entered or where he went ; he did not want to be disturbed.

He roused himself during a long journey to take a drink of something held to his lips by someone, and sank back, tucking sleep around him like a warm blanket.

In all his life he had never had such a gorgeous sleep as that, his weary and harassed brain revelled in moments of semi-consciousness, and then sank back into the last abysms of oblivion.

He awoke a new man, physically and mentally, and with an absolutely clear memory and understanding. He awoke in a bedroom—a cheerful bedroom—lit by the morning sun, a bedroom with an open window, through which came the songs of birds and the whisper of foliage.

A young man dressed in a black morning-coat was seated in an arm-chair by the window, reading a book. He looked like a superior sort of servant.

Jones looked at this young man, who had not yet noticed the awakening of the sleeper ; and Jones, as he looked at him, put facts together.

Simms, Cavendish, the fact that he had been doped, the place where he was, and the young man. He had been taken here in that conveyance, whatever it was ; they had thought him mad ; they had carted him off to a madhouse, this was a madhouse, that guy in the chair was an attendant. He recognized these probabilities very clearly, but he felt no anger and little surprise. His mind, absolutely set up and almost renewed by profound slumber, saw everything clearly and in a true light.

It was quite logical that, believing him mad, they had put him in a madhouse, and he had no fear at all of the result, simply because he knew that he was sane. The situation was amusing, it was also one to get free from ; but there was plenty of time, and there was no room for making mistakes.

Curiously enough, now, the passionate, or almost passionate, desire to recover his own personality had vanished, or, at least, was no longer active in his mind ; his brain, renewed by that tremendous sleep, was no longer tainted by that vague dread, no longer troubled by that curious craving to have others believe in his story and to have others recognize him as Jones.

No, it did not matter to him just now whether he recovered his personality in the eyes of others ; 'what did matter to him was the recovery of his bodily freedom. Meanwhile, caution. Like Brer Rabbit, he determined to " lie low."

" Say," said Jones.

The young man by the window started slightly, rose, and came to the bedside.

" What o'clock ? " said the patient.

" It has just gone half-past eight, sir," replied the
other. " I hope you have slept well."

Jones noticed that this person did not " my lord "
him.

" Not a wink," said he. " Tossed and tumbled all
night. Oh, say, what do *you* think——"

The young man looked puzzled.

" And would you like anything now, sir ? "

" Yes, my pants. I want to get up."

" Certainly, sir ; your bath is quite ready," replied
the other.

He went to the fireplace and touched an electric
button, then he bustled about the room getting Jones's
garments together.

The bedroom had two doors, one leading to a sitting-
room, one to a bath-room ; in a minute the bath-
room door opened and a voice queried, " Hot or
cold ? "

" Hot," said Jones.

" Hot," said the attendant.

" Hot," said the unseen person in the bath-room,
as if registering the order in his mind. Then came
the fizzling of water, and in a couple of minutes the
voice :

" Gentleman's bath ready."

Jones bathed, and though the door of the bath-
room had been shut upon him, and there was no
person present, he felt all the time that someone was
watching him. When he was fully dressed, the
attendant opened the other door and ushered him
into the sitting-room, where breakfast was laid on
a small table by the window. He had the choice
between eggs and bacon and sausages ; he chose the
former, and, whilst waiting, and attracted by the

pleasant summery sound of croquet balls knocking
together, he looked out of the window.

Two gentlemen in white flannels were playing
croquet, stout, elderly gentlemen they were, and on
a garden-seat a young man in flannel trousers and a
grey tweed coat was seated, watching the game and
smoking cigarettes.

He guessed these people to be fellow-prisoners.
They looked happy enough, and, having noticed this
fact, he sat down to breakfast.

He noted that the knife accompanying his fork
was blunt and of very poor quality—of the sort
warranted not to cut throats—but he did not heed
much. He had other things to think of. The men
in flannels had given him a shock. Instinctively he
knew them to be "inmates." He had never considered the question of lunatics and lunatic asylums
before. Vague recollections of Edgar Allan Poe
and the works of Charles Reade had surrounded the
term lunatic asylum with an atmosphere of feather
beds and brutality, the word lunatic conjured up in
his mind the idea of a man obviously insane. The
fact that this place was a house quite ordinary and
pleasant in appearance, and these sane-looking gentlemen, lunatics, gave him a grue.

The fact that an apparently sane individual can
be held as a prisoner was beginning to steal upon him ;
that a man might be able to play croquet, and laugh
and talk and take an intelligent interest in life, and yet,
just because of some illusion, be held as a prisoner.

He did not fully realize this yet, but it was dawning
upon him. But he did fully realize that he had lost
his liberty.

Before he had finished his eggs and bacon this
recognition became acute.

The fear of losing his own personality had vanished utterly, all that haunting dread was gone. If he could escape now, so he told himself, he would go right back to the States. He had eight thousand pounds in the National Provincial Bank ; no one knew that it was there. He could seize it with a clear conscience, and take it to Philadelphia. The shadow of Rochester —oh, that was a thing gone for ever, dissipated by this actual fact of lost liberty—so he told himself.

A servant brought up the *Times*, and he opened it and lit a cigarette.

Then, as he looked casually over the news and the doings of the day, an extraordinary feeling came upon him. All this printed matter was relative to the doings and ideas of free men, men who could walk down the street if the fancy pleased them. It was like looking at the world through bars. He got up and paced the floor ; the breakfast-things had been removed, and the attendant had left the room and was in the bedroom adjoining.

Jones walked softly to the door through which the servant had carried away the things, and opened it gently and without noise. A corridor lay outside, and he was just entering it, when a voice from behind made him turn :

" Do you require anything, sir ? "

It was the attendant.

" Nothing," said Jones. " I was just looking to see where this place led to."

He came back into the room.

He knew now that every movement of his was watched, and he accepted the fact without comment. He sat down and took up the *Times*, whilst the attendant went back to the bedroom.

He had said to himself on awaking that a sane

man, held as insane, could always win free just by his sanity.   He was taking up this line of reasoning now, and casting about him for a method.

He was not long in finding one.   The brilliancy of the idea that had all at once struck him made him cast the paper from his knees to the floor.   Then, having smoked a cigarette and consolidated his plan, he called the attendant.

" I want to see the gentleman who runs this place."

" Dr. Hoover, sir ? "

" Yes."

" Certainly, sir, I will ring and have him sent for."

He rang the bell ; a servant answered and went off with the message.

Jones took up the paper again and resumed his cigarette.   Five minutes passed, and then the door opened and a gentleman entered.

A pleasant-faced, clean-shaven man of fifty, dressed in blue serge and with a rose in his button-hole, such was Dr. Hoover.   But the eye of the man held him apart from others—a blue-grey eye, keen, sharp, hard, for all the smile upon the pleasant face.

Jones rose up.

" Dr. Hoover, I think," said he.

" Good morning," said the other in a hearty voice. " Fine day, isn't it ?   Well, how are we this morning ? "

" Oh, I'm all right," said Jones.   " I want to have a little talk with you."

He went to the bedroom door, which was slightly ajar, and closed it.

" For your sake," said Jones, " it's just as well we have no one listening ;   the attendant is in there— you are sure he cannot hear what we say, even with the door shut ? "

" Quite," said Hoover, with a benign smile.

He was used to things like this, profoundly confidential communications concerning claims to crowns and principalities or grumbles about food.

He did not expect what followed.

" I am not going to grumble at your having me here," said Jones ; " it's my fault for playing practical jokes. I didn't think they'd go the length of doping me and locking me up under the name I gave them."

" And what name was that ? " asked Hoover kindly.

" Jones."

" Oh, and now tell me, if you are not Mr. Jones, who are you ? "

" Who am I—well, I can excuse the question. I'm the Earl of Rochester."

This was a nasty one for Hoover, but that gentleman's face showed nothing.

" Indeed," said he ; " then why did you call yourself Jones ? "

" For a joke ; I slung them a yarn, and they took it in. Then they gave me a draught to compose my nerves ; they thought really that I was dotty, and I drank it—you must have seen the condition I was in when I got here."

" Hum, hum ! " said Hoover.

He was used to the extremely cunning ways of gentlemen off their balance, and he had a profound belief in Simms and Trapson, whose names endorsed the certificate of lunacy he had received with the newcomer. He was also a man just as cunning as Jones.

" Well," he said, with an air of absolute frankness, " this takes me by surprise—a practical joke ; but why did you play such a practical joke ? "

" I know," said Jones, " it was stupid, just a piece of tomfoolery ; but you see how I am landed."

Dr. Hoover ignored this evasion whilst noting it.

Then he began to ask all sorts of little questions, seemingly irrelevant enough. Did Jones think that he was morally justified in carrying out such a practical joke ? Why did he not say at once it was a practical joke, after the affair had reached a certain point ? Was his memory as good as of old ? Was he sure in his own mind that he was the Earl of Rochester ? Was he sure that, as the Earl of Rochester, he could hold that title against a claim that he was not the earl ? Give details, and so forth ?

" Now, suppose," said Dr. Hoover, " I were to con-test the title with you, and say, ' You are Mr. Jones and I am the Earl of Rochester,' how would you estab-lish your claim ? I am simply asking to find out whether what you consider to be a practical joke was, in fact, a slight lapse of memory on your part—a slight mind disturbance such as is easily caused by fatigue or over-work, and which often leaves effects lasting some weeks or months.

" Now, I must point out to you that, as—practical joke or not—you came here calling yourself Mr. Jones, I would be justified in asking you for proof that you are *not* Mr. Jones. See my point ? "

" Quite."

" Well, then, prove your case," said the physician jovially.

" How can I ? "

" Well, if you are the Earl of Rochester, let me test your memory. Who is your banker ? "

" Coutts."

Hoover did not know who the Earl of Rochester's banker might be, but the promptness of the reply satisfied him of its truth, the promptness was also an index of sanity. He passed at a venture to a subject on which he was acquainted.

" And how many brothers and sisters have you ? "

That was fatal.

Jones's eye fell under the pressure of Hoover's.

" There is no use in going on with these absurd questions," said he, " a thing everyone knows."

" But I just want to prove to you," said Hoover gently, " that your mind, which in a week from now will have quite recovered, is still a little bit shaky. Now, how long is it since you succeeded to the title —it's just a test memory question."

Jones did not know. He saw that he was lost. He had also gained an appreciation of Hoover. Beside the fat Simms and the cadaverous Cavendish, Hoover seemed a man of keen common sense.

Jones recognized that the new position into which he had strayed was a blind alley. If he were detained until his memory could answer questions of which his mind knew nothing, he would be detained for ever. He came to the grand determination to try back.

" Look here," said he, " let's be straight with one another. I can't answer your questions. Now, if you are a man of sense, as I take you to be, and not a man like those others, who think everyone but themselves is mad, you will recognize *why* I can't answer your questions. I'm not Rochester. I thought I'd get out of here by pretending that I'd played a practical joke on those guys—it was a false move, I acknowledge it ; but when I fixed on the idea, I didn't know the man I had to deal with. If you will listen to my story, I will tell you in a few words how all this business came about."

" Go on," said Hoover.

Jones told, and Hoover listened, and when the tale was over, at the end of a quarter of an hour or so, Jones scarcely believed it himself. It sounded crazy. Much more crazy than when he had told it to the Duke of Melford, and the reason of this difference was Hoover. There was something in Hoover's eye, something in his make up and personality, something veiled and critical, that destroyed confidence.

"I have asked them to make inquiries," finished Jones. "If they will only do that, everything will be cleared up."

"And you may rest content we will," said Hoover.

"Now for another thing," said Jones. "Till I leave this place, which will be soon, I hope, may I ask you to tell that confounded attendant not to be always watching me. I don't know whether you think me mad or sane ; think me mad, if you like, but take it from me, I'm not going to do anything foolish, but if anything would drive me crazy, it would be feeling that I am always being watched like a child."

Hoover paused a moment. He had a large experience of mental cases. Then he said :

"You will be perfectly free here. You can come downstairs and do as you like. We have some very nice men staying here, and you are free to amuse yourself. I'll just ask you this, not to go outside the grounds till your health is perfectly established. This is not a prison ; it's a sanatorium. Colonel Hawker is here for gout, and Major Barstowe for neuritis ; got it in India. You will like them. There are several others who make up my household—you can come on down with me now. Are you a billiard-player ? "

"Yes, I can play ; but, see here, before we go down, where is this place ? I don't even know what part of the country it's in."

" Sandbourne-on-Sea," replied Hoover, leading the way from the room.

*   *   *   *

Now, in London on the night before, something had happened.   Dr. Simms, at a dinner-party given by Dr. Took, of Bethlem Hospital, had, relative to the imagination of lunatics, given an instance :

" Only to-day," said Simms, " I had a case in point. A man gave me as his supposed address one thousand one hundred and one, Walnut Street, Philadelphia."

" But there is a Walnut Street, Philadelphia," said Took, " and it's ten miles long, and the numbers run up well towards that."

Half an hour later, Simms got into his carriage.

" Savoy Hotel, Strand," said he to the coachman.

CHAPTER IX

SIMMS, in his electric brougham, passed through the gas-lit streets in the direction of the Strand, glancing at the night pageant of London, but seeing nothing.

I love to linger over Simms, but what pages of description could adequately describe him ?—buxom, sedate, plump and soothing, with the appearance of having been born and bred in a frock-coat, above all things discreet. You can fancy him stepping out of his brougham, passing into the hall of the hotel and presenting his card to the clerk, with a request for an interview with the manager. The manager being away, his deputy supplied his place.

" Yes, an American gentleman of the name of Jones had stayed in the hotel, and on the night of the first of June had met with " an accident " on the Underground Railway. The police had taken charge of the business. What address had he given when booking his room ? An address in Philadelphia. Walnut Street, Philadelphia."

" Thanks," said Simms. " I came to inquire because a patient of mine fancied, seeing the report, that it might be a relative. She must have been mistaken, for her relative resides in the city of New York. Thank you—quite so—good evening."

In the hall Simms hesitated for a moment, then he asked a page-boy for the American bar, found it, and ordered a glass of soda-water.

There were only one or two men in the bar, and, as Simms paid for his drink, he had a word with the bar-tender.

" Did he remember some days ago seeing two gentlemen in the bar who were very much alike ? "

The bar-tender did, and as an indication how in huge hotels dramatic happenings may pass unknown to the staff not immediately concerned, he had never connected Jones with the American gentleman of whose unhappy demise he had read in the papers.

He was quite free in his talk. The likeness had struck him forcibly, never seen two gentlemen so like one another, dressed differently, but still like. His assistant had seen them, too.

" Quite so," said Simms, " they are friends of mine, and I hoped to see them again here this evening— perhaps they are waiting in the lounge."

He finished his soda-water and walked off. He sought the telephone office and rang up Curzon Street.

The Duke of Melford had dined at home, but had gone out. He was at the Buffs' Club in Piccadilly.

Simms drove to the Club.

The Duke was in the library.

His Grace had literary leanings. His " History of the Siege of Bundlecund," of which seven hundred copies of the first edition remained unsold, had not deterred him from attempting the " Siege of Jutjutpore." He wrote a good deal in the library of the club, and to-night he was in the act of taking down some notes on the character of Fooze Ali, the leader of the besiegers, when Simms was announced.

The library was deserted by all save the historian, and getting together into a cosy corner, the two men talked.

" Your Grace," said Simms, " we have made a

mistake. Your nephew is dead, and that man we have placed with Dr. Hoover is what he announced himself to be."

" What ! What ! What ! " cried the duke.

" There can be no doubt at all," said Simms. " I have made inquiries."

He gave details. The duke listened, his narrow brain incensed at this monstrous statement that had suddenly risen up to confront it.

" I don't believe a word of it ! " said he, when the recital was over, " and what's more, I won't believe it ! Do you mean to tell me I don't know my own nephew ? "

" It's not a question of that," said Simms. " It's just a question of the facts of the case. There is no doubt at all that a man exactly like the late—your nephew, in fact, stayed at this hotel, that he there met the—your nephew. There is no doubt that this man gave the address to the hotel people he gave to us, and there is no doubt in my mind that he could make out a very good case if he were free. That there would be a very great scandal—a world scandal. Even if he were not to prove his case the character of—your nephew—would be held up for inspection. Then again, he would have very powerful backers. Now you told me of this man Mulhausen. How would that property stand were this man to prove his claim, and prove that Lord Rochester was dead when the transfer of the property was to be made to him ? I am not thinking of my reputation," finished the ingenuous Simms, " but of your interests, and I tell you quite plainly, your Grace, that were this man to escape we would all be in a very unpleasant predicament."

" Well, he won't escape," said the duke. " I'll see to that."

" Quite so, but there is another matter. The Commissioners in Lunacy."

" Well, what about them ? "

" It is the habit of the Commissioners to visit every establishment registered under the Act, and unfortunately, they are men—I mean, of course, that, fortunately, they are men of the most absolute probity, but given to overriding sometimes the considered opinion of those in close touch with the cases they are brought in contact with. They would undoubtedly make strict inquiries into the truth of the story that Lord Rochester has just put up, and the result—I can quite see it—would drift us into one of those *exposés*, those painful and interminable lawsuits, destructive alike to property, to dignity, and that ease of mind inseparable from health and the enjoyment of those positions to which my labours and your Grace's lineage entitle us."

" Damn the Commissioners ! " suddenly broke out his Grace. " Do you mean to say they would doubt my word ? "

" Unfortunately, it is not a question of that," said Simms. " It is a question of what they call the liberty of the subject."

" Damn the liberty of the subject—liberty of the subject ! When a man's mad, what right has he to liberty—liberty to cut people's throats, maybe ? Look at that fool Arthur—liberty ! Look at the use he made of his liberty when he had it. Look what he did to Llangwathby—sent a telegram leading him to believe that his wife had broken out again—you know how she drinks—and had been gaoled in Carlisle. And the thing was so artfully constructed. It said almost nothing. You couldn't touch him on it. Simply said, ' Go at once to police court Carlisle.'

See the art of it ? Never mentioned the woman's name. There was no libel. Llangwathby, to prosecute, would have to explain all about his wife. He went. What happened ? You know his temper. He went to Llangwathby Castle before going to the police court, and the first person he saw was his wife. Before all the servants ! Before all the servants, mind you, he said to her, ' So they have let you out of prison and now you'd better get out of my house ! ' You know her temper. Before all the servants ! Before all the servants, mind you, she accused him of that disgraceful affair in Pont Street, when he was turned out in his pyjamas—and they half ripped off him, by Lord Tango's brother. Tango never knew anything of it. Never would, but he knows now, for Lucy Jerningham was at Llangwathby when the scene occurred, and she's told him. The result is poor Llangwathby will find himself in the D. C.—Liberty, what right has a man like that to talk of liberty ? "

" Quite so," said Simms, utterly despairing of pressing home the truth of the horrible situation upon this brain in blinkers. " *Quite* so. But facts are facts, and the fact remains that this man—I mean—er— Lord Rochester, possesses, on your own showing, great craft and subtlety. And he will use that with the Commissioners in Lunacy when they call."

" When do they call ? "

" Ah, that's just it. They visit asylums and registered houses at their own will, and the element of surprise is one of their methods. They may arrive at Hoover's any time. I say, literally, any time. Sometimes they arrive at a house in the middle of the night, they may leave an asylum unvisited for a month and then come twice in one week, and they hold everyone concerned, literally, in the hollows of their hands.

If denied admittance they would not hesitate to break the doors down.   Their power is absolute."

" But, good God, sir ! " cried the duke, " what you tell me is monstrous !   It's un-English.   Break into a man's house, spy upon him in the middle of the night !   Why, such powers vested in a body of men make for terrorization.   This must be seen to.   I will speak about it in the House."

" Quite so, but, meanwhile, there is the danger, and it must be faced."

" I'll take him away from Hoover's."

" Ah ! " said Simms.

" I'll put him somewhere where these fellows won't be able to interfere.   How about my place at Skibo ? "

Simms shook his head.

" He is under a certificate," said he.   " The Commissioners call at Hoover's, inspect the books, find that Lord Rochester has been there, find him gone, find you have taken him away.   They will simply call upon you to produce him."

" How about my yacht ? " asked the other.

" A long sea voyage for his health ? "

" Ah ! " said Simms, " that's better ; but voyages come to an end."

" How about my villa at Naples ?   Properly looked after there, he will be safe enough."

" Of course," said Simms, " that will mean he will always have to be there—always."

" Of course, always.   D'you think now I have got him in safety I will let him out ? "

Simms sighed.   The business was drifting into very dangerous waters.   He knew for a matter of fact, and also by intuition, that Jones was Jones, and that Rochester was dead, and his unfortunate position was like this :

1. If Jones escaped from Hoover's unsoothed and furious, he might find his way to the American consul, or, *horror!* to some newspaper office. Then the band would begin to play.

2. If Jones were transferred on board the duke's yacht and sequestrated, the matter at once became *criminal,* and the prospect of long years of mental distress and dread lest the agile Jones should break free stood before him like a nightmare.

3. It was impossible to make the duke believe that Jones was Jones, and that Rochester was dead.

The only thing to be done was to release Jones, soothe him, bribe him and implore of him to get back to America as quick as possible.

This being clear before the mind of Simms, he at once proceeded to act.

" It is not so much the question of your letting him out," said he, " as of his escaping. And now I must say this. My professional reputation is at stake, and I must ask you to come with me to Curzon Street and put the whole matter before the family. I wish to have a full consultation."

The duke demurred for a moment. Then he agreed, and the two men left the club.

At Curzon Street they found the Dowager Countess and Venetia Birdbrook about to retire for the night. Teresa, Countess of Rochester, had already retired, and, though invited to the conference, refused to leave her room.

Then in the drawing-room with closed doors, Simms, relying on the intelligence of the women as a support, began, for the second time, his tale.

He convinced the women, and by one o'clock in the morning, still standing by his guns after the fashion of the defenders of Bundlecund, the duke had to confess

that he had no more ammunition. Surrendered, in
fact.

" But what is to be done ? " asked the distracted
mother of the defunct. " What will this terrible man
do if we release him ? "

" Do ? " shouted the duke. " Do ?—why the impostor may well ask what will we do to him ! "

" We can do nothing," said Venetia. " How can
we ?   How can we expose all this before the servants—
and the public ?   It is all entirely Teresa's fault.   If
she had treated Arthur properly none of this would
ever have happened.   She laughed and made light of
his wickedness, she——"

" Quite so," said Simms, " but, my dear lady, what
we have to think of now is the man Jones.   We must
remember that whilst being an extremely astute person, inasmuch as he recovered for you that large property from the man Mulhausen, he seems honest.
Indeed, yes, it is quite evident that he is honest.   I
would suggest his release to-morrow and the tendering
to him of an adequate sum, say, one thousand pounds,
on the condition that he retires to the States.   Then,
later, we can think of some means to account for the
demise of the late Earl of Rochester, or simply leave it
that he has disappeared."

The rest of this weird conclave remains unreported,
Simms, however, carrying his point and departing
next day, after having seen his patients, for Sandbourne-on-Sea, where he arrived late in the afternoon.

When the hired fly that carried him from Sandbourne Station arrived at the Hoover establishment,
it found the gate wide open, and at the gate one of the
attendants standing in an expectant attitude, glancing
up and down the road, as though he were looking for
something, or waiting for somebody.

CHAPTER X

SMITHERS

HOOVER, leading the way downstairs, showed Jones the billiard-room on the first floor, the dining-room, the smoke-room. All pleasant places, with windows opening on the gardens. Then he introduced him to some gentlemen. To Colonel Hawker, just come in from an after-breakfast game of croquet ; to Major Barstowe ; and to a young man, with no chin to speak of, named Smithers. There were several others, very quiet people ; the three mentioned are enough for consideration.

Colonel Hawker and Major Barstowe were having an argument in the smoking-room when Hoover and Jones entered.

" I did not say I did not believe you," said Barstowe. " I said it was strange."

" Strange ! " cried the colonel. " What do you mean by strange ? It's not the word I object to, it's the tone you spoke in."

" What's the dispute ? " asked Hoover.

" Why," said Barstowe, " the colonel was telling me he had seen pigs in Burmah sixteen feet long and sunflowers twenty feet in diameter."

" Oh, that story," said Hoover. " Yes, there's nothing strange in that."

" I'll knock any man down that doubts my word ! "
said the colonel. " That's flat."

Hoover laughed ; Jones shivered.

Then the disputants went out to play another game
of croquet, and Jones, picking up with Smithers,
played a game of billiards, Hoover going off and leaving
them alone.

After playing for about five minutes, Smithers, who
had maintained an uncanny silence, broke off the game.

" Let's play something better than this," said he.
" Did you know I was rich ? "

" No," said Jones.

" Well, I'm very rich. Look here." He took nine
sovereigns from his pocket and showed them with pride.
" I play pitch and toss with these," said he. " Hoover
doesn't mind so long as I don't lose them. Pitch and
toss with sovereigns is fine fun ; let's have a game."

Jones agreed.

They sat on the divan and played pitch and toss.
At the end of ten minutes Jones had won twenty
pounds.

" I think I will stop now," said Smithers. " Give
me back that sovereign I lent you to toss with."

" But you owe me twenty pounds," said Jones.

" I'll pay you that to-morrow," said Smithers.
" These sovereigns are not to be spent ; they are only
for playing with."

" Oh, that doesn't matter," said Jones, handing
back the coin, and recognizing that, penniless as he
was, here was a small fund to be drawn upon by cunning, should he find a means of escape. " I'm rich.
I'm worth ten millions."

" Ten million sovereigns ? "

" Yes."

" Golden ones, like these ? "

" Yes."

" I say," said Smithers, " could you lend me one or two ? "

" Yes, rather."

" But you mustn't tell Hoover."

" Of course I won't."

" When will you lend me them ? "

" When I get my bag of sovereigns from London. They are coming down soon."

" I like you," said Smithers. " We'll be great friends, won't we ? "

" Rather.   Come out in the garden."

They went out.

The garden encircled the house ; big wrought iron gates, locked, gave upon the road.

The tennis and croquet lawns lay at the back of the house ; brick walls, covered in part with fruit-trees, surrounded the whole place. The wall on the left of the house struck Jones as being practicable, and he noticed that none of the walls were spiked or glassed. Hoover's patients were evidently not of the dangerous and agile type.

" What's at the other side of this wall ? " asked Jones, as they passed on by the left-hand barrier.

Smithers giggled.

" Girls," said he.

" Girls !   What sort of girls ? "

" Little ones with long hair, and bigger ones. They learn their lessons there ; it's a school. The gardener left his ladder there one day, and I climbed up. There was a lot of girls there. I nodded to them, and they all came to the wall. I made them all laugh. I asked them to come over the wall and toss for sovereigns—then a lady came and told me to go away. She didn't seem to like me."

Jones, all during luncheon—the meal was served in his own apartments—revolved things in his mind, Smithers amongst others. Smither's mania for handling gold had evidently been satisfied by giving him these few coins to play with. They were real ones; Jones had satisfied himself of that. Smithers, despite his want of chin, was evidently not a person to be put off with counterfeit coins. Jones had come down from London dressed just as he had called at Curzon Street. That is to say, in a black morning coat and grey trousers. His tall hat had evidently been forgotten by his deporters. After luncheon he asked for a cap to wear in the garden, and was supplied with a grey tweed shooting-cap of Hoover's.

With this on his head he took his seat in an arbour, an arbour which, he noticed, had its opening facing the house.

Here, smoking, he continued revolving his plans, and here afternoon tea was served to him.

Ten minutes later the colonel and the major began another game of croquet, and five minutes after that came from the house Smithers, with a butterfly-net in his hand.

Jones left the arbour and joined Smithers.

" The sovereigns have come," said Jones.

" The bag of sovereigns ? "

" Yes ; with a big red seal from the bankers. I'm going to give you fifty."

" Oh, lord ! " said Smithers. " But you haven't said anything to Hoover ? "

" Not a word. But you must do something for me before I give you them."

" What's that ? "

" I want you to go up to Colonel Hawker, and take him aside."

" Yes ? "

" And tell him that Major Barstowe says he's a liar."

" Yes ? "

" That's all."

" That's easy enough," said Smithers.

" I'll stand by the wall here, and if any of the girls look over, as they probably will, for I'm going to whistle to them, I'll make them come over and toss for sovereigns."

" That would be a lark," said the unfortunate.

" Bother," said Jones, " I've forgot ! "

" What ? "

" All my sovereigns are upstairs in the bag. I know ; lend me yours whilst I'm waiting."

" I—I never lend sovereigns," said Smithers.

" Why ? I'm going to *give* you fifty, and I only ask you to lend me yours for a moment, in case those girls——"

Smithers put his hand in his pocket and produced the coins ; they were in a little chamois leather bag.

" Don't open the bag," said he, " just shake it, and they'll know there are sovereigns in it by the noise."

" Right ! " said Jones. " Now go and tell Colonel Hawker that Major Barstowe says he's a liar."

Smithers went off, butterfly-net in hand.

Jones was under no delusion. He reckoned that the garden was always under surveillance, and that a man getting over a wall would have little chance of reaching the street unless he managed to distract the attention of watchers. He thought it probable that his conversation with Smithers had been seen, and possibly the handing over of some article noted.

There was a seat just here, close to the wall. He sat down on it, pulled his cap over his eyes, and stretched out his legs. Then, under the peak of the cap, he watched Smithers approach Colonel Hawker, interrupt him just as he was on the point of making a stroke, and lead him aside.

The effect on the colonel's mind of the interruption to his stroke, followed by the sudden information that his veracity had been impeached, was miraculous and sudden as the slap on the side of the face that sent the butterfly-hunter flying. The attack on Barstowe, who seemed to fight well, the cries, the shouts, the imprecations, the fact that half a dozen people, inmates and attendants, joined in the confusion as if by magic, all this was nothing to Jones, nor was the subsidiary fact that one of the inmates, a quiet-mannered clergyman with a taste for arson, had taken advantage of the confusion, and was patiently and sedulously at work firing the thatch of the summer-house in six different places with a long-concealed box of matches.

Jones, on the stroke of the colonel, had risen from the seat, and, with the aid of a well-trained plum-tree, had reached the top of the wall and dropped on the other side into a bed of mignonette. It was a hockey day at the school, and there were no girls in the garden. He ran across it to the open front gate and reached the road, ran down the road, which was deserted and burning in the late afternoon sunshine, reached a side road and slackened his pace. All the roads were of the same pattern, broad, respectable, and lined with detached and semi-detached houses set in gardens, and labelled according to the owner's fancy. Old Anglo-Indian colonels and majors lived here, and one knew their houses by such names as " Lucknow," " Cawnpore," etc., just as one knows azaleas by their blossoms. Jones, like an animal making for cover, pushed on till he reached a street of shops. A long, long street, running north and south, with the shop fronts on the eastern side, sun-blinded and sunlit. A peep of blue and perfect sea showed at the end of the street, and on the sea the white sail of a boat. Sandbourne-on-Sea is a pleasant place to stay at, but Jones did not want to stay there.

His mind was working feverishly. There was sure to be a railway station somewhere, and, as surely, the railway station would be the first place they would hunt for him.

London was his objective. London and the National Provincial Bank, but of the direction or the distance to be travelled he knew no more than the man in the moon.

CHAPTER XI

A S the fox seeks an earth he was seeking for a hole to hide in. Across the road a narrow house, set between a fishmonger's shop and a seaside library, displayed in one of its lower windows a card with the word "Apartments." Jones crossed the road to this house and knocked at the hall door. He waited a minute and a half, ninety seconds, and every second a framed vision of Hoover in pursuit, Hoover and his assistants streaming like hounds on a hot scent. Then he found a decrepit bell and pulled it.

Almost on the pull the door opened, disclosing a bustless, sharp-eyed and cheerful-looking little woman of fifty or so, wearing a cameo brooch and cornelian rings. She wore other things, but you did not notice them.

" Have you rooms to let ? " asked Jones.

" Well, sir, I have the front parlour unoccupied," replied the landlady, " and two bedrooms on the top floor. Are there any children ? "

" No," said Jones. " I came down here alone for a holiday. May I see the rooms ? "

She took him to the top front bedroom first. It was clean and tidy, just like herself, and gave a cheery view of the shop fronts on the opposite side of the street.

Jones, looking out of the window, saw something that held him for a moment fascinated and forgetful of his surroundings and his companion. Hoover, no less, walking hurriedly and accompanied by a man who looked like a gardener. They were passing towards the sea, looking about them as they went. Hoover had the appearance of a person who has lost a purse or some article of value, so Jones thought as he watched them vanish. He turned to the landlady.

" I like this room," said he, " it is cheerful and quiet, just the sort of place I want. Now let's see the parlour."

The parlour boasted of a horsehair sofa, chairs to match, pictures to match, and a glass-fronted book-case containing volumes of the " Sunday Companion," " Sword and Trowel," " Home Influence," and Ouida's " Moths " in the old, yellow-back, two-shilling edition.

" Very nice indeed," said Jones.   " What do you charge ? "

" Well, sir," said the landlady—her name was Henshaw—" it's a pound a week for the two rooms without board, two pounds with."

" Any extras ? " asked the artful Jones.

" No, sir."

" Well, that will do me nicely. I came along here right from the station, and my portmanteau hasn't arrived, though it was labelled for here, and the porter told me he had put it on the train. I'll have to go up to the station this evening again to see if it has arrived. Meanwhile, seeing I haven't my luggage with me, I'll pay you in advance."

She assured him that this was unnecessary, but he insisted.

When she had received the money she asked him what he would have for supper, or would he prefer late dinner ?

" Supper," replied Jones, " oh, anything. I'm not particular."

Then he found himself alone. He sat down on the horsehair sofa to think. Would Hoover circularize his description and offer a reward ? No, that was highly improbable. Hoover's was a high-class establishment, he would avoid publicity as much as possible, but he would be pretty sure to use the intelligence, such as it was, of the police, telling them to act with caution.

Would he make inquiries at all the lodging-houses ? That was a doubtful point. Jones tried to fancy himself in Hoover's position and failed.

One thing certainly Hoover would do. Have all the exits from Sandbourne-on-Sea watched. That was the logical thing to do, and Hoover was a logical man.

There was nothing to do but give the hunt time to cool off, and at this thought the prospect of days of lurking in this room of right angles and horsehair-covered furniture, rose up before him like a black billow. Then came the almost comforting thought, he could not lurk without creating suspicion on the part of Mrs. Henshaw. He would have to get out, somehow. The weather was glorious, and the strip of seaweed hanging by the mantelpiece dry as tinder. A sea-side visitor who sat all day in his room in the face of such weather, would create a most unhealthy interest in the mind of any sea-side landlady. No, whatever else he might do he could not lurk.

The most terrible things in dramatic situations are the little things that speak to one for once in their lives. The pattern of the carpet that tells you that there is no doubt of the fact that your wife has run away with all your money, and left you with seven children to look after ; the form of the chair that tells you that Justice with a noose in her hand is waiting on the front door step. Jones, just now, was under the obsession of *the* picture of the room, whose place was above the mantelpiece.

It was an oleograph of a gentleman in uniform, probably the Prince Consort, correct, sane, urbane— a terrible companion for a man in an insane situation ; for insanity is not confined to the brain of man or its productions—though heaven knows she has a fine field of movement in both.

A thundering rat-tat-tat at the hall door brought Jones to his feet. He heard the door answered, a voice outside saying " N'k you," and the door shut. It was some parcel left in. Then he heard Mrs. Henshaw descending the kitchen stairs and all was quiet. He turned to the bookcase, opened it, inspected the contents, and chose " Moths."

CHAPTER XII

" MOTHS "

I N ill-health or convalescence, or worry or tribulation, the ordinary mind does not turn to Milton or Shakespeare, or even the sermons of Charles Haddon Spurgeon. There are few classics that will stand the test of a cold in the head, or a fit of depression, or a worrying husband, or a minor tragedy. Here the writer of " light fiction " stands firm.

Jones had never been a great reader; he had read a cheap novel or two, but his browsings in the literary fields had been mainly confined to the uplands where the grass is improving.

Colour, poetry, and construction in fiction were unknown to him, and now—he suddenly found himself on the beach at Trouville.

On the beach at Trouville, with Lady Dolly skipping before him in the sea.

He had reached the forced engagement of the beautiful heroine to the wicked Russian Prince, when the door opened and the supper tray entered, followed by Mrs. Henshaw. Left to honour and her own initiative, she had produced a huge lobster, followed by cheese, and three little dull-looking jam-tarts on a willow-pattern plate.

When Jones had ruined the lobster and devoured the

199

tarts he went on with the book. The lovely heroine had become for him Teresa, Countess of Rochester; the opera singer himself, and the Russian Prince Maniloff.

Then the deepening dusk tore him from the book. Work had to be done.

He rang the bell, told Mrs. Henshaw that he was going to the railway station to see after his luggage, took his cap, and went out. Strangely enough, he did not feel nervous. The first flurry had passed, and he had adapted himself to the situation; the deepening darkness gave him a sense of security, and the lights of the shops cheered him somehow.

He turned to the left towards the sea.

Fifty yards down the street he came across a gentlemen's outfitter's, in whose windows coloured neckties screamed, and fancy shirts raised their discordant voices with gents' summer waistcoats and those panama hats, adored in the year of this story by the river and sea-side youth.

Jones, under the hands of Rochester's valet, and forced by circumstances to use Rochester's clothes, was one of the best-dressed men in London. Left to himself in this matter he was lost. He had no idea of what to wear, or what not to wear, no idea of the social damnation that lies in tweed trousers not turned up at the bottom, fancy waistcoats, made evening ties, a bowler worn with a black morning coat, or dog-skin gloves. Heinenberg and Obermann of Philadelphia had dressed him till Stultz unconsciously took the business over. He was barely conscious of the incongruity of his present get-up topped by the tweed shooting-cap of Hoover's, but he was quite conscious of the fact that some alteration in dress was imperative as a means towards escape from Sandbourne-on-Sea.

He entered the shop of Towler and Simpkinson, bought a six-and-elevenpenny panama, put it on and had the tweed cap done up in a parcel. Then a flannel coat attracted him. A grey flannel tennis coat, price fifteen shillings. It fitted him to a charm, save for the almost negligible fact that the sleeves came down nearly to his knuckles. Then he bought a night-shirt for three-and-eleven, and had the whole lot done up in one parcel.

At a chemist's next door he bought a tooth-brush. In the mirror across the counter he caught a glimpse of himself in the panama. It seemed to him that not only had he never looked so well in any other head-gear, but that his appearance was completely altered.

Charmed and comforted, he left the shop. Next door to the chemist's and at the street corner was a public-house.

Jones felt certain from his knowledge of Hoover, that the very last place to come across one of his assistants would be a public-house. He entered the public bar, took a seat by the counter, and ordered a glass of beer and a packet of cigarettes. The place was rank with the fumes of cheap tobacco and cigarettes, and the smell of beer. Hard gas light showed no adornment, nothing but pitch pine panelling, spittoons, bottles on shelves and an almanac. The barmaid, a long-necked girl with red hands, and cheap rings and a rose in her belt, detached herself from earnest conversation with a youth in a bowler inhabiting the saloon bar, pulled a handle, dumped a glass of beer before Jones and gave him change without word or glance, returning to her conversation with the bowlered youth. She evidently had no eyes at all for people in the public bar. There are grades, even in the tavern.

Close to where Jones had taken his seat was standing
a person in broken shoes, an old straw hat, a coat
with parcels evidently in the tail pockets, and trousers
frayed at the heels. He had a red, unshaven face,
and was reading the *Evening News*.

Suddenly he banged the paper with the tips of the
fingers of his right hand and cast it on the counter.

"Govinment! Govinment! nice sort of govinment, payin' each other four hundred a year for
followin' Asquith and robbin' the landowners to get
the money—God lumme!"

He paused to light a filthy clay pipe. He had his
eyes on Jones, and evidently considered him, for some
occult reason, of the same way of political thinking
as himself, and he addressed him in that impersonal
way in which one addresses an audience.

"They've downed and outed the House o' Lords,
an' now they're scraggin' the Welsh Church, after
that they'll go for the landed prepriotor and finish
him. And who's to blame? The Radicals—no, they
ain't to blame, no more than rats for their instincts;
we're to blame, the Conservatives is to blame; we
haven't got a fightin' man to purtect us. The Radicals
has got all the tallant—you look at the fight Bonna
Lor's been makin' this week. Fight! A blind tom
cat with his head in an old t'marter tin would make
a better fight than Bonna Lor's put up. Look at
Churchill, that chap was one of us once; he was born
to lead the clarses, an' now look at him leadin' the
marses, up to his neck in Radical dirt, and pretendin'
he likes it. He doesn't, but he's a man with an
eye in his head, and he knows what we are, a boneless
lot without organization. I say it myself, I said it
only larst night in this here bar, and I say it again,
for two pins I'd chuck my party. I would so. For

two pins I'd chuck the country, and leave the whole
lot to stew in their own grease."

He addressed himself to his beer, and Jones, greatly
marvelling, lit a cigarette.

" Do you live here ? " asked he.

" Sh'd think I did," replied the other. " Born
here and bred here, and been watchin' the place
going down for the last twenty years, turnin' from a
decent residential neighbourhood to a collection of
schools and lodgin' houses, losin' clarse every year.
Why, the biggest house here is owned by a chap that
sells patent food; there's two socialists on the town
council, and the Mayor last year was Hoover, a chap
that owns a lunatic 'sylum. One of his loonies
got out last March and near did for a child on the
Southgate Road before he was collared ; and yet
they make a Mayor of him."

" Have another drink ? " said Jones.

" I don't mind if I do."

" Well, here's luck," said he, putting his nose into
the new glass.

" Luck ! " said Jones. " Do Hoover's lunatics
often escape ? "

" Escape—why I heard only an hour ago another
of them was out. Gawd help him if the town folk
catch him at any of his tricks, and Gawd help Hoover.
A chap has no right comin' down and settin' up a
business like that in a place like this, full of nurse-
maids and children. People bring their innercent
children down here to play on the sands, and any
minit that place may break loose like a bum-shell.
That's not marked down on the prospectices they
publish with pictures done in blue and yaller, and lies
about the air and water, and the salubriarity of the
South coast."

" No, I suppose not," said Jones.

" Well, I must be goin'," said the other, emptying his glass, and wiping his mouth on the back of his hand.   " Good night to you."

" Good night."

The upholder of Church and State shuffled out, leaving Jones to his thoughts.   Wind of the business had got about the town, and even at that moment, no doubt, people were carefully locking back doors, and looking in out-houses.

It was unfortunate that the last man to escape from the Hoover establishment had been violently inclined; that was the one thing needed to stimulate Rumour and make her spread.

Having sat for ten minutes longer and consumed another glass of tepid beer, he took his departure.

Mrs. Henshaw let him in, and having informed her of his journey to the station, the fruitlessness of his quest, and his opinion of the railway company, its servants and its methods, he received his candle and went to bed.

CHAPTER XIII

A TRAMP, AND OTHER THINGS

HE was awakened by a glorious morning, and, looking out of his window, he saw the street astir in the sunshine, stout men in white flannels with morning newspapers in their hands, children already on their way to the beach with spades and buckets, all the morning life of an English sea-coast town in summer.

Then he dressed. He had no razor, his beard was beginning to show, and to go about unshaved was impossible to his nature. For a moment the wild idea of letting his beard grow—that oldest form of disguise—occurred to him, only to be dismissed immediately. A beard takes a month to grow; he had neither the time nor the money to do it, nor the inclination.

At breakfast—two kippered herrings and marmalade—he held a council of war with himself.

Nature has equipped every animal with means for offence and defence. To man she has given daring, and that strange indifference in cool blood to danger, when danger has become familiar, which seems the attribute of man alone.

Jones determined to risk everything, go out,

prospect, find some likely road of escape, and make a bold dash. The eight thousand pounds in the London Bank shone before him like a galaxy of eight stars ; no one knew of its existence. What he was to do when he had secured it was a matter for future consideration. Probably he would return right away to the States.

One great thing about all this Hoover business was the fact that it had freed him from the haunting dread of those terrible sensations of duality and negation. Fighting is the finest antidote to nerve troubles and mental dreads, and he was fighting now for his liberty, for the fact stood clearly before him that, whether the Rochester family believed him to be Rochester or believed him to be Jones, it was to their interest to hold him as a lunatic in peaceful retirement.

Having breakfasted, he lit a cigarette, asked Mrs. Henshaw for a latch-key so that he might not trouble her, put on his panama and went out. There was a barber's shop across the way ; he entered it, found a vacant chair, and was shaved. Then he bought a newspaper, and strolled in the direction of the beach. The idea had come to him that he might be able to hire a sailing boat and reach London that way ; a pre- posterous and vague idea that still, however, led him till he reached the esplanade, and stood with the sea wind blowing in his face.

The only sailing boats visible were excursion craft, guarded by longshoremen, loading up with trippers, and showing placards to allure the innocent.

The sands were swarming, and the bathing machines crawling towards the sea.

He came on to the beach and took his seat on the warm, white sands with freedom before him had he been a gull or a fish. To take one of those cockle-shell row boats and scull a few miles down the coast would lead him where? Only along the coast, rock-strewn beyond the sands and faced with cliffs. Of boat craft he had no knowledge, the sea was choppy, and the sailing boats now out seemed going like race horses over hurdles.

No, he would wait till after luncheon, then in that somnolent hour, when all men's thoughts are a bit dulled, and vigilance least awake, he would find some road, on good, hard land, and make his dash.

He would try and get a bicycle map of this part of Wessex. He had noticed a big stationer's and bookseller's near the beach, and he would call there on his way back.

Then he fell to reading his paper, smoking cigarettes, and watching the crowd.

Watching, he was presently rewarded with the sight of the present day disgrace of England. Out of a bathing tent, and into the full sunlight, came a girl with nothing on, for skin-tight blue stockinette is nothing in the eyes of Modesty: every elevation, every depression, every crease in her shameless anatomy exposed to a hundred pairs of eyes, she walked calmly towards the water. A young man to match followed. Then they wallowed in the sea.

Jones forgot Hoover. He recalled Lady Dolly in " Moths." Lady Dolly, who, on the beach of Sand-bourne-on-Sea would have been the pink of propriety, and the inhabitants of this beach were not wicked society people, but respectable middle-class folk.

" That's pretty thick," said Jones to an old gentle-man like a goat sitting close to him, whose eyes were fixed in contemplation on the bathers.

" What ? "

" That girl in blue. Don't any of them wear decent clothes ? "

" The scraggy ones do," replied the other, speaking in a far-away and contented manner.

At about half-past eleven Jones left the beach, tired of the glare and the bathers, and the sand-digging children. He called at the book-shop, and for a shilling obtained a bicycle map of the coast, and sitting on a seat outside the shop, scanned it.

There were three roads out of Sandbourne-on-Sea : the London road ; a road across the cliffs to the west, and a road across the cliffs to the east. The easterly road led to Northbourne, a seaside town some six or seven miles away ; the westerly road to Southbourne, some fifteen miles off. London lay sixty miles to the north. The railway touched the London road at Houghton Admiral, a station some nine miles up the line.

That was the position. Should he take the London road and board a train at Houghton Admiral, or take the road to Northbourne and get a train from there ?

The three ways lay before him like the three Fates, and he determined on the London road.

However, Man proposes and God disposes.

He folded up the map, put it in his pocket and started for home—or, at least, Mrs. Henshaw's.

Just at the commencement of the street he paused before a photographer's to inspect the pictures exposed for view. Groups, family parties, children, and girls with undecided features. He turned from the contemplation of these things, and found himself face to face with Hoover.

Hoover must have turned into the street from a by-way, for only sixty seconds before the street had been Hooverless. He was dressed in a Norfolk

-jacket and knickerbockers, and his calves showed huge.

" Hello ! " said Jones.

The exclamation was ejected from him, so to speak, by the mental shock.

Hoover's hand shot out to grasp his prey. What happened then was described by Mr. Shonts, the German draper across the way, to a friend.

" Der thin man hit Mr. Hoover in the stomack, who sat down, but lifted himself at wance and pursued him."

Jones ran. After him followed a constable, sprung from nowhere, boys, a dog that seemed running for exercise, and Hoover.

He reached the house of Mrs. Henshaw, pulled the latch-key from his pocket, plunged it in the lock, opened the door and shut it. So close was the pursuit on him that the ' bang-bang ' of the knocker followed at once on the bang of the door.

Then the bell went, peal after peal.

Jones made for the kitchen stairs and bolted down them, found a passage leading to the back door, and, disregarding the bewildered Mrs. Henshaw, who was coming out of the kitchen with her hands all over flour, found the backyard.

A blank wall lay before him, another on the right, and another on the left. The left and right walls divided the Henshaw backyard from the yards of the houses on either side; the wall immediately before him divided it from the backyard of a house in Minerva Terrace, which was parallel to the High Street.

Jones chose this wall. A tenantless dog-kennel standing before it helped him, and next moment he was over, shaken up with a drop of twelve feet and facing a clothes-line full of linen. He dived under a sheet and almost into the back of a broad woman hanging linen on a second clothes-line, found the back door of the house, which the broad woman had left open, ran down a passage, up a kitchen stairs and into a hall. An old gentleman in list slippers, coming out of a room on the right, asked him what he wanted. Jones, recalling the affair later, could hear the old gentleman's voice and words.

He did not pause to reply. He opened the hall door, and the next moment he was in Minerva Terrace. It was fortunately deserted. He ran to the left, found a by-way and a terrace of artisans' dwellings, new, hideous, and composed of yellow brick. In front of the terrace lay fields. A gate in the hedge invited him ; he climbed over it, crossed a field, found another gate which led him to another field, and found himself surrounded by the silence of the country—a silence pierced and thrilled by the songs of larks. Larks make the sea lands of the south and east coasts insufferable. One lark in a suitable setting, and, for a while, is delightful, but twenty larks in all grades of ascent and descent, some near, some distant, make for melancholy.

Jones crouched in a hedge for a while to get back his breath. He was lost. Road maps were not much use to him here. The larks insisted on that, jubilantly or sorrowfully, according to the stage of their flight.

Then something or someone immediately behind him on the other side of the hedge breathed a huge sigh, as if lamenting over his fate. He jumped up. It was a cow. He could see her through the brambles and smell her, too, sweet as a Devonshire dairy.

Then he sat down again to think and examine the

map, which he had fortunately placed in his pocket. The roads were there, but how to reach them was the problem, and the London road, to which he had pinned his faith, was now impossible. It would be surely watched. He determined, after a long consultation with himself, to make for Northbourne, striking across the fields straight ahead, and picking up the cliff road somewhere on its course.

He judged, and rightly enough, that Hoover would hunt for him, not along the coast, but inland. Northbourne was not the road to London, even though a train might be caught from Northbourne. The whole business was desperate, but his course seemed the least desperate way out of it. And he need not hurry; speed would be of no avail in this race against Fate.

He took the money from his pocket and counted it. Out of the nine pounds he started with from Hoover's there remained only five pounds eleven and ninepence. He had spent as follows :

		£	s.	d.
Mrs. Henshaw	.. ..	2	0	0
Panama	..		6	11
Nightshirt	..		3	11
Coat..	..		15	0
Public-house ..	..			10
Shave and newspaper	..			7
Road map	..		1	0
		£3	8	3

He went over these accounts and checked them in his head. Then he put the money back in his pocket and started on his way across the fields.

Despite all his worries, this English country interested him; it also annoyed him. Fields, the size of pocket handkerchiefs, divided one from the other by monstrous hedges and deep ditches. To cross this country in a straight line one would want to be a deer or a bounding kangaroo. Gates, always at corners and always diagonal to his path, gave him access from one field to the other. There were few trees. The English tree has an antipathy to the sea, and keeps away from it, but the hedge has no sensitiveness of this sort. These hedges seemed to love the sea, to judge by their size.

He was just in the act of clambering over one of the innumerable gates when a voice hailed him. He looked back. A young man in leggings, who had evidently been following him unperceived, raised a hand. Jones finished his business with the gate, and then, with it between him and the stranger, waited. He was well-dressed in a rough way, evidently a superior sort of farmer, and physically a person to be reckoned with. He was also an exceedingly cantankerous-looking individual.

" Do you know that you are trespassing ? " asked he, when they were within speaking distance.

" No," said Jones.

" Well, you are. I must ask you for your name and address, please."

" What on earth for—what harm am I doing your old fields ? " Jones had forgotten his position, everything, before the outrage on common sense.

" You are trespassing, that's all. I must ask you for your name and address."

Now to Jones came the recollection of something he had read somewhere. A statement that in England there was no law of trespass in the country places,

and that a person might go anywhere to pick mush-
rooms or wild flowers, and no landlord could interfere
so long as no damage was done.

"Don't you know the law?" asked Jones. He
recited the law accordingly to the Unknown.

The other listened politely.

"I ask you for your name and address," said he.
"Our lawyers will settle the other matter."

Then anger came to Jones.

"I am the Earl of Rochester," said he, "and my
address is Carlton House Terrace, London. I have
no cards on me."

Then the queerest sensation came to Jones, for he
saw that the other had recognized him. Rochester
was evidently as well known to the ordinary English-
man, by picture and repute, as Lloyd George.

"I beg your pardon," said the other, "but the fact
is, my land is overrun with people from Sandbourne
—sorry."

"Oh, don't mention it," replied the Earl of
Rochester. "I shan't do any damage. Good day."
They parted, and he pursued his way.

A mile farther on he came upon a person with
broken boots, a beery face, and clothes to match his
boots. This person was seated in the sunshine under
a hedge, a bundle and a tin can beside him.

He hailed Jones as "Guvernor," and requested a
match.

Jones supplied the match, and they fell into
conversation.

"Northbourne," said the tramp. "I'm goin' that
way meself. I'll show you the quickest way when
I've had a suck at me pipe."

Jones rested for a moment by the hedge whilst
the pipe was lit. The trespass business was still hot

in his mind. The cave-in of the landlord had not entirely removed the sense of outrage.

" Aren't you afraid of being had up for trespass ? " asked he.

" Trespass," replied the other, " not me. I ain't afeared of no farmers."

Jones gave his experience.

" Don't you be under no bloomin' error," said the tramp, when the recital was finished. " That chap was right enough. That chap couldn't touch the likes of me, unless he lied and swore I'd broke fences ; but he could touch the likes of you. I know the lor. I know it in and out. Landlords don't know it as well as me. That chap knows the lor, else he wouldn't 'a' been so keen on gettin' your name and where you lived."

" But how could he have touched me if he cannot touch you ? "

The tramp chuckled.

" I'll tell you," said he, " and I'll tell you what he'll do now he's got where you live. He'll go to the Co't o' Charncery and arsk for a 'junction against you to stop you goin' over his fields. You don't want to go over his fields any more, that don't matter. He'll get his 'junction, and you'll have to pay the bloomin' costs—see—the bloomin' costs, and what will that amahnt to ? Gawd knows, maybe a hundred pound. Lots of folks take it into their silly heads they can go where they want. They carnt, not if the landlord knows his lor, not unless they're hoofin' it like me. Lot o' use bringin' *me* up to the Co't o' Charncery."

" Do you mean to say that just for walking over a field a man can be had up to the Court of Chancery and fined a hundred pounds ? "

" He ain't fined, it's took off him in costs."

" You seem to know a lot about the law," said Jones, calling up the man of the public-house last night, and coming to the conclusion that amongst the English lower orders there must be a vast fund of a peculiar sort of intelligence.

" Yus," said the tramp. " I told you I did." Then, interestedly, " What might your name be ? "

Jones repeated the magic formula to see the effect.

" I am the Earl of Rochester."

" Lord Rawchester. Thought I knew your face. Lost half a quid over your horse runnin' at Gatwood Park last spring twel' months. ' White Lady ' came in second to ' The Nun.' Half a quid. I'd made a bit on ' Champane Bottle ' in the sellin' plate. Run me eye over the lists and picked out ' White Lady.' Didn't know nothin' abaht her ; said to a fren' : ' Here's my fancy. Don't know nothin' abaht her, but she's one of Lord Rawchester's, an' his horses run stright.' That's what I said, ' His horses run stright,' and give me a stright run hoss with a wooden leg before any of your fliers with a dope in his belly or a pullin' jockey on his back. But the grown' did her : she was beat on the post by haff an 'eck, you'll remember. She'd 'a' won be two lengths, on'y for that bit o' soggy grown' be the post. That grown' wants overhaulin' ; haff a shower o' rain, and a hoss wants fins and flippers instead o' hoofs."

" Yes," said Jones, " that's so."

" A few barra' loads o' gravel would put it rite," continued the other. " It ain't fair on the hosses, and it ain't fair on the backers. 'Arf a quid I dropped on that mucky bit o' grown'. Last Doncaster meetin' I was sayin' the very same thing to Lor' Lonsdale over the Doncaster course. I met him, man to man like, outside the ring, and he handed me out a cigar. We talked same as you and me might be talkin' now, and I says to him : ' What we want's more money put into drains on the courses. Look at them mucky farmers, the way they drains their land,' says I, ' and look at us runnin' hosses and layin' our bets and let down, hosses and backers and all, for want of the courses bein' looked after proper.' "

He tapped the dottle out of his pipe, picked up the bundle, and rose grumbling.

Then he led the way in the direction of Northbourne.

It was a little after three o'clock now, and the day was sultry. Jones, despite his other troubles, was vastly interested in his companion. The height of Rochester's position had never appeared truly till shown him by the farmer and this tramp. They knew him. To them, without any doubt, the philosophers and poets of the world were unknown, but they knew the Earl of Rochester, and not unfavourably.

Millions upon millions of the English world were equally acquainted with his lordship ; he was most evidently a National figure. His unconventionality, his " larks," his lavishness, and his horse-racing propensities, however they might pain his family, would be meat to the legions who loved a lord, who loved a bet, who loved a horse, and a picturesque spendthrift.

To be Rochester was not only to be a lord, it was more than that. It was to be famous, a national character, whose picture was printed on the retina of the million. Never had Jones felt more inclined to stick to his position than now, with the hounds on his traces, a tramp for his companion, and darkness ahead. He felt that if he could once get to London, once lay his hands on that eight thousand pounds lying in the National Provincial Bank, he could fight. Fight for freedom, get lawyers to help him, and retain his phantom coronet.

He had ceased to fear madness; all that dread of losing himself had vanished, at least, for the moment. Hoover had cured him.

Meanwhile they talked as they went, the tramp laying down the law as to rights over commons and waste lands, seeming absolutely to forget that he was talking to, or supposed to be talking to, a landed proprietor. At last they reached the white ribbon that runs over the cliffs from Sandbourne to Northbourne and beyond.

" Here's the road," said the tramp, " and I'll be takin' leave of your lor'ship. I'll take it easy for a bit amongst them bushes; there's no call for me to hurry. I shawnt forget meetin' your lor'ship. Blimy if I will. Me sittin' there under that hedge an' thinkin' of that half quid I dropped over ' White Lady,' and your lor'ship comin' along—it gets me ! "

Up to this moment of parting he had not once Lordshipped Jones.

Jones, feeling in his pocket, produced the half-sovereign, which, with five pounds one and ninepence, made up his worldly wealth at the moment.

He handed it over, and the tramp spat on it for luck.

Then they parted, and the fugitive resumed his way with a lighter pocket but a somewhat lighter heart.

There are people who increase and people who reduce one's energy; it is sometimes enough to look at them without even talking to them. The tramp belonged to the former class. He had cheered Jones. There was nothing particularly cheery in his conversation; all the same, the effect had been produced.

Now, along the cliff road and coming from the direction of Northbourne a black speck developed, resolving itself at last into the form of an old man carrying a basket. The basket was filled with apples and Banbury cakes. Jones bought eight Banbury cakes and two apples with his one and ninepence, and then took his seat on the warm turf by the way to devour them. He lay on his side as he ate and cursed Hoover.

To lie here for an hour on this idyllic day, to watch the white gulls flying, to listen to the whisper of the sea far below, what could be better than that ? He determined if ever he should win freedom and money to return here for a holiday.

He was thinking this, when, raised now on his elbow, he saw something moving amongst the bushes and long grass of the waste lands bordering the cliff road.

It was a man, a man on all fours, yet moving swiftly, a sight natural enough in the deer-stalking Highlands, but uncanny on these Wessex downs.

Jones, leaving four Banbury cakes uneaten on the grass, sprang to his feet, so did the crawling one.

Then the race began.

The pursuer was handicapped.

Any two sides of a triangle are longer than the third. A right line towards Jones would save many yards, but the going would be bad on account of the brambles and bushes ; a straight line to the road would lengthen the distance to be covered, but would give a much better course when the road was reached. He chose the latter.

The result was, that when the race really started the pursuer was nearly half a mile to the bad. But he had not recently consumed four Banbury cakes and two apples. Super-Banbury cakes of the dear old days,

when margarine was ninepence a pound, flour un-
limited, and currants unsought after by the wealthy.

Jones had not run for years. And in this connection it is quite surprising how Society pursues a man
once he gets over the barrier—and especially when he
has to run for his liberty.

The first mile was bad, then he got his second wind
handed to him, despite everything, by a fair constitu-
tion and a fairly respectable life, but the pursuer was
now only a quarter of a mile behind. Up to this the
course had been clear, with no spectators, but now came
along from the direction of Northbourne an invalid
on the arm of an attendant, and behind them a boy on
a bicycle. The bicycle was an inspiration.

It was also yellow-painted, and bore a carrier in
front blazoned with the name of a Northbourne
Italian warehouseman. It contained parcels, evidently
intended for one of the few bungalows that strewed
the cliff.

The boy fought to defend his master's property,
briefly, but still he fought, till a happy stroke in the
wind laid him on the sun-warmed turf. The screams
of the invalid—it was a female—sounded in the ears
of Jones like part of some fantastic dream, so seemed
the bicycle. It had no bell, the saddle wanted raising
at least two inches; still, it went, and the wind was
behind.

On the right was a sheer drop of two hundred feet,
and the road here skirted the cliff edge murderously
close, for the simple reason that cliff falls had eaten the
bordering grass to within a few feet of the road. This
course, on an unknown and questionable bicycle laden
with parcels of tea and sugar, was open to a good many
objections; they did not occur to Jones, he was making
good speed, or thought he was till the long declivity

leading to Northbourne was reached. Here he began
to know what speed really was, for he found on pressing
the lever that the brake would not act. Fortunately
it was a free wheel.

This declivity runs between detached villas and stone
walls, sheltering prim gardens, right on to the west
end of the esplanade, which is, in fact, a continuation
of it. For the first few hundred yards Jones thought
that nothing could go quicker than the houses and walls
rushing past him ; towards the end he was not thinking.

The esplanade opened out, a happy band of children
with buckets and wooden spades, returning home to
tea, opened out, gave place to rushing apartment
houses with green balconies on the left, rushing sea-
scape and bathing-machines on the right. Then the
speed slackened.

He got off, shaking, and looked behind him. He
had reached the east end of the promenade. It lay,
as it always lies towards five o'clock, absolutely deserted
by visitors. In the distance and just stepped out of a
newspaper kiosk a woman was standing, shading her
eyes and looking towards him. Two boatmen near
her were looking in the same direction. They did not
seem excited, just mildly interested.

At that moment appeared on the long slope leading
down to the esplanade the figure of a man running.
He looked like a policeman—a seaside policeman.

Jones did not pause to verify. He propped the
bicycle against the rails of a verandahed house and
ran.

The esplanade at this, the eastern end, ascends
to the town by a zig-zag road. As he took this ascent
the mind of Jones, far from being clouded or dulled,
was acutely active. It saw that now the railway station of Northbourne was out of count ; flight by train

was impossible, for the station was the very first place that would be watched ; the coast line, to judge by present results, was impossible, for it seemed that to keep to it he might go on for ever being chased till he reached John o' Groats.

Northbourne is the twin image of Sandbourne-on-Sea, the same long High Street, the same shops with blinds selling the same wares, the same trippers, children with spades, and invalids.

The two towns are rivals, each claiming the biggest brass band, the longest esplanade, the fewer deaths from drowning, the best drains, the most sunlight, and the swiftest trains from London. Needless to say that one of them is not speaking the truth, a fact that does not seem to disturb either of them in the least.

Jones, walking swiftly, passed a seaside boot-shop, a butcher's, greengrocer's, and Italian warehouse— the same, to judge by the name over the door—that had sent forth the messenger-boy on the bicycle. Then came a cinema palace, with huge pictures splashed across with yellow bands, announcing :

" TO-NIGHT."

Then a milliner's, then a post-office, and lastly a livery stables.

In front of the latter stood a char-à-banc nearly full. A black board announced in white chalk : " Two hours' drive, two shillings," and the congregation in the char-à-banc had that stamp. Stout women, children, a weedy man or two, and a honeymoon couple.

Jones, without the slightest hesitation, climbed into the char-à-banc. It seemed sent by Heaven. It was a seat, it went somewhere, and it was a hiding-place. Seated amongst these people he felt intuitively that a viewless barrier lay between him and his pursuers; that it was the very last place a man in search of a runaway would glance at.

He was right. Whilst the char-à-banc still lingered on the chance of a last customer, the running police-man—he was walking now—appeared at the sea end of the street. He was a young man with a face like an apple, he wore a straw helmet—Northbourne serves out straw helmets for its police and straw hats for its horses on the first of June each year—and he seemed blown. He was looking about him from right to left, but he never looked once at the char-à-banc and its contents. He went on, and round the corner of the street he vanished, still looking about him.

A few moments later the vehicle started. The contents were cheerful and communicative one with the other, conversing freely on all sorts of matters, and Jones, listening despite himself, gathered all sorts of information on subjects ranging from the pictures then exhibiting at the cinema palace, to the price of butter.

He discovered that the contents consisted of three family parties—exclusive of the honeymoon couple—and that the appearance of universal fraternity was deceptive, that the parties were exclusive, the conver-sation of each being confined to its own members.

So occupied was his mind by these facts that they were a mile and a half away from Northbourne and in the depths of the country before a great doubt seized him.

He called across the heads of the others to the driver, asking where they were going to.

" Sandbourne-on-Sea," said the driver.

Now, though the Sandbournites hate the Northbourn-ites as the Guelphs the Ghibellines, though the two

towns are at advertisemental war, the favourite pleasure drive of the chars-à-bancs of Sandbourne is to
Northbourne, and vice versa. It is chosen simply
because the road is the best thereabouts, and the
gradients the easiest for the horses.

" Sandbourne-on-Sea ? " cried Jones.

" Yes," said the driver.

The vision of himself being carted back to Sandbourne-on-Sea with that crowd and then back again
to Northbourne—if he were not caught—appeared to
Jones for the moment as the last possible grimace of
Fate. He struggled to get out, calling to the driver
that he did not want to go to Sandbourne. The
vehicle stopped, and the driver demanded the full fare
—two shillings. Jones produced one of his sovereigns,
but the man could not make change, neither could any
of the passengers.

" I'll call at the livery stables as I go back," said
Jones, " and pay them there."

" Where are you stayin' in the town ? " asked the
driver.

" Belinda Villa," said Jones.

It was the name of the villa against whose rails he
had left the bicycle. The idiocy of the title had
struck him vaguely at the moment, and the impression
had remained.

" Mrs. Cass ? "

" Yes."

" Mrs. Cass's empty."

This unfortunate condition of Mrs. Cass did not floor
Jones.

" She was yesterday," said he, " but I have taken
the front parlour and a bedroom this afternoon."

" That's true," said a fat woman ; " I saw the
gentleman go in with his luggage."

In any congregation of people you will always find a liar ready to lie for fun, or the excitement of having a part in the business on hand; failing that, a person equipped with an imagination that sees what it pleases.

This amazing statement of the fat woman almost took Jones's breath away. But there are other people in a crowd beside liars.

" Why can't the gentleman leave the sovereign with the driver and get the change in the morning ? " asked one of the weedy-looking men. This scarecrow had not said a word to anyone during the drive. He seemed born of mischance to live for that supreme moment, diminish an honest man's ways of escape, and wither.

Jones withered him.

" You shut up," said he. " It's no affair of yours— cheek ! " Then to the driver : " You know my address ; if you don't trust me you can come back with me and get change."

Then he turned and walked off, whilst the vehicle drove on.

He waited till a bend of the road hid it from view, and then he took to the fields on the left.

He had still the remains of the packet of cigarettes he had brought at Sandbourne, and, having crossed four or five gates, he took his seat under a hedge and lit a cigarette.

He was hungry. He had done a lot of work on four Banbury cakes and an apple.

CHAPTER XIV

THE ONLY MAN IN THE WORLD WHO WOULD BELIEVE HIM

THE tobacco took the edge from his desire for food, increased his blood pressure, and gave rest to his mind.

He sat thinking. The story of " Moths " rose up before his mind, and he fell to wondering how it ended and what became of the beautiful heroine with whom he had linked Teresa, Countess of Rochester, of Zouroff, with whom he had linked Maniloff, of Corréze, with whom he had linked himself.

The colour of that story had tinctured all his seaside experiences. Then Mrs. Henshaw rose up before his mind. What was she thinking of the lodger who had flashed through her life and vanished over the back garden wall? And the interview between her and Hoover—that would have been well worth seeing. Then the boy on the bicycle and the screaming invalid rose before him, and that mad rush down the slope of the esplanade ; if those children with spades and buckets had not parted as they did, if a dog had got in his way, if the slope had ended in a curve ! He amused himself with picturing these possibilities and their results ; and then all at once a drowsiness more delightful than any dream closed on him and he fell asleep.

It was after dark when he awoke, with the remnant of a moon lighting the field before him. From far away and borne on the wind from the sea came a faint sound as of a delirious donkey with brass lungs braying at the moon. It was the sound of a band. The Northbourne brass band playing in the Cliff Gardens above the moonlit sea. Jones felt to see that his cigarettes and matches were safe in his pocket, then he started, taking a line across country, trusting in Providence as a guide.

Sometimes he paused and rested on a gate, listening to the faint and indeterminate sounds of the night, through which came occasionally the barking of a distant dog, like the beating of a trip hammer.

It was a perfect summer's night, one of those rare nights that England alone can produce ; there were glow-worms in the hedges and a scent of new-mown hay in the air. Though the music of the band had been blotted out by distance, listening intently, he caught the faintest suspicion of a whisper, continuous, and evidently the sound of the sea.

An hour later, that is to say towards eleven o'clock, weary with finding his way out of fields into fields, into grassy lanes and around farm-house buildings, desperate, and faint from hunger, Jones found a road, and by the road a bungalow with a light in one of the windows.

A dauntingly respectable-looking bungalow in the midst of a well laid-out garden.

Jones opened the gate and came up the path. He was going to demand food, offer to pay for it if necessary, and produce gold as an evidence of good faith.

He came into the verandah, found the front door, which was closed, struck a match, found the bell, pulled and pulled it. There was no response. He waited a little and then rang again, with a like result. Then he came to the lighted window.

It was a French window, only half closed, and a half turned-down lamp showed a comfortably furnished room and a table laid out for supper.

Two places were set. A cold fowl intact on a dish garnished with parsley stood side by side with a York ham the worse for wear, a salad, a roll of cowslip-coloured butter, a loaf of home-made bread and a cheese tucked around with a snow-white napkin made up the rest of the eatables, whilst a decanter of claret shone invitingly by the seat of the carver. There was nothing wanting, or only the invitation.

The fowl supplied that.

Jones pushed the window open and entered. Half closing it again, he took his seat at the table, placing his hat on the floor beside him. Taking a sovereign from his pocket, he placed it on the white cloth. Then he fell to.

You can generally tell a man by his claret, and judging from this claret, the unknown who had supplied the feast must have been a most estimable man.

A man of understanding and parts, a man not to be deluded by specious wine lists, a generous, warm-hearted and full-blooded soul—and here he was.

A step sounded on the verandah, the window was pushed open, and a man of forty years or so, well-dressed, tall, thin, dark and saturnine, stood before the feaster.

He showed no surprise. Removing his hat, he bowed.

Jones half rose.

" Hello," said he confusedly, with his mouth full —then he subsided into his chair.

" I must apologize for being late," said the tall man, placing his hat on a chair, rubbing his long hands together and moving to the vacant seat. " I was unavoidably detained. But I'm glad you did not wait supper."

He took his seat, spread his napkin on his knees, and poured himself out a glass of claret. His eyes were fixed on the sovereign lying upon the cloth. He had noted it from the first. Jones picked it up and put it in his pocket.

" That's right," said the unknown. Then, as if in reply to a question : " I will have a wing, please."

Jones cut a wing of the fowl, placed it in the extra plate which he had placed on one side of the table, and presented it. The other cut himself some bread, helped himself to salad, salt and pepper, and started eating, absolutely as though nothing unusual had occurred or was occurring.

For half a minute or so neither spoke. Then Jones said :

" Look here," said he, " I want to make some explanations."

" Explanations," said the long man ; " what about ? "

Jones laughed.

" That sovereign which I put on the table, and which I have put back in my pocket. I must apologize. Had I gone away before you returned, that would have been left behind to show that your room had been entered neither by a hobo nor a burglar, nor by some cad who had committed an impertinence—perhaps you will believe that."

The long man bowed.

" But," went on Jones, " by a man who was driven by circumstance to seek hospitality without invitation."

The other had suddenly remembered the ham, and had risen and was helping himself, his pince-nez, which he wore on a ribbon and evidently only for reading purposes, dangling against his waistcoat buttons.

" By circumstance," said he; " that is interesting. Circumstance is the master dramatist—are you interested in the Drama ? "

" Interested ! " said Jones. " Why, I *am* a drama. I reckon I'm the biggest drama ever written, and that's why I am here to-night."

" Ah," said the other, " this is becoming more interesting still, or promising to become, for I warn you, plainly, that what may appear of intense interest to the individual is generally of little interest to the public. Now, a man may, let's say, commit some little act that the thing we call Justice disapproves of, and eluding Justice, find himself pressed by Circumstance into queer and dramatic positions; those positions, though of momentary and intense interest to the man in question, would be of the vaguest interest to the man in the stalls or the girl eating buns in the gallery, unless they were connected by that thread of—what shall we call it— that is the backbone of the thing we call Story."

" Oh, Justice isn't bothering after me," said Jones. Then vague recollections began to stir in his mind: that long, glabrous face, the set of that jaw, that forehead, that hair, brushed back.

" Why, you're Mr. Kellerman, aren't you ? " said he.

The other bowed.

" Good heavens ! " said Jones, " I ought to have known you. I've seen your picture often enough in the States, and your cinema plays—haven't read your books, for I'm not a reading man—but I've been fair crazy over your cinema plays."

Kellerman bowed.

" Help yourself to some cheese," said he ; " it's good. I get it from Fortnum and Mason's. When I stepped into this room and saw you here, for the first moment I was going to kick you out, then I thought I'd have some fun with you and freeze you out. So you're American ? You are welcome. But just tell me this. Why did you come in, and how ? "

" I came in because I am being chased," said Jones; " it's not the law, I reckon I'm an honest citizen—in purpose, anyhow, and as to how I came in, I wanted a crust of bread and rang at your hall door."

" Servants don't sleep here," said Kellerman. " Cook snores—bungalow like a fiddle for conveying sounds—come here for sleep and rest. They sleep at a cottage down the road."

" So ? " said Jones. " Well, getting no reply, I looked in at the window, saw the supper, and came in."

" That's just the sort of thing that might occur in a photo play," said Kellerman. " When I saw you, as I stepped in, sitting quietly at supper, the situation struck me at once."

" You call that a situation," said Jones ; " it's bald to some of the situations I have been in for the last God knows how long."

" You interest me," said Kellerman, helping himself to cheese. " You talk with such entire conviction of the value of your goods."

" How do you mean, the value of my goods ? "

" Your situations, if you like the term better. Don't you know that good situations are rarer than diamonds, and more valuable ?   Have you ever read Pickwick ? "

" Yep."

" Then you can guess what I mean. Situations don't occur in real life ; they have to be dug for in the diamond fields of the mind, and——"

" Situations don't occur in real life ! " said Jones. " Don't they.   Now, see here, I've had supper with you, and in return for your hospitality I'll tell you everything that's happened to me if you'll hear it. I guess I'll shatter your illusions. I'll give you a sample : I belong to the London Senior Conservative Club, and yet I don't. I have the swellest house in London, yet it doesn't belong to me. I'm worth one million and eight thousand pounds, yet the other day I had to steal a few sovereigns, but the law could not touch me for stealing them. I have an uncle who is a duke, yet I am no relation to him.   Sounds crazy, doesn't it ; all the same it's fact. I don't mind telling you the whole thing if you care to hear it.   I won't give you the right names because there's a woman in the case, but I bet I'll lift your hair."

Kellerman did not seem elated.

" I don't mind listening to your story," said he, " on one condition."

" What's that ? "

" That you will not be offended if I switch you off if the thing palls, and hand you your hat, for I must tell you that though I came down here to get sleep, I do most of my sleeping between two in the morning and noon. I work at night, and I had intended working to-night."

" Oh, you can switch me off when you like," said Jones.

Supper being finished, Kellerman fastened the window, and, carrying the lamp, led the way to a comfortably furnished study. Here he produced cigars, and put a little kettle on a spirit stove to make tea.

Then, sitting opposite to his host, in a comfortable arm-chair, Jones began his story.

He had told his infernal story so often that one might have fancied it a painful effort, even to begin. It was not. He had now an audience in touch with him. He suppressed names, or rather altered them, substituting Manchester for Rochester, and Birdwood for Birdbrook. The audience did not care, it recked nothing of titles, it wanted Story—and it got it.

At about one o'clock the recital was interrupted whilst tea was made, at two o'clock or a little after the tale finished.

" Well ? " said Jones.

Kellerman was leaning back in his chair with eyes half closed ; he seemed calculating something in his head.

" Do you believe me ? "

Kellerman opened his eyes.

" Of course I believe you. If you had invented all that, you would be clever enough to know what your invention is worth, and not hand it out to a stranger. But I doubt whether anyone else will believe you—however, that is your affair—you have given me five reels of the finest stuff, or, at least, the material for it, and if I ever care to use it I will fix you up a contract giving you twenty-five per cent. royalties. But there's one thing you haven't given me—the *dénouement*. I'm more than interested in that. I'm not thinking of money ; I'm a film actor at heart, and I want to help in the play. Say, may I help ? "

" How ? "

" Come along with you to the end, give all the assistance in my power—or even without that, just watch the show. I want to see the last act, for I'm blessed if I can imagine it."

" I'd rather not," said Jones. " You might get to know the real names of the people I'm dealing with, and as there is a woman in the business, I don't feel I ought to give her name away even to you. No. I reckon I'll pull through alone, but if you'd give me a sofa to sleep on to-night I'd be grateful. Then I can get away in the morning."

Kellerman did not press the point.

" I'll give you better than a sofa," he said. " There's a spare bed, and you'd better not start in the morning ; give them time to cool down. Then towards evening you can make a dash ; the servants here are all right, they'll think you are a friend run down from town to see me. I'll arrange all that."

CHAPTER XV

PEBBLEMARSH

AT five o'clock next day, Jones, re-dressed by Kellerman in a morning coat rather the worse for wear—a coat that had been left behind at the bungalow by one of Kellerman's friends—and a dark cloth cap, took his departure from the bungalow. His appearance was frankly abominable, but quite distinct from the appearance of a man dressed in a grey flannel tennis coat and wearing a panama—and that was the main point.

Kellerman had also worked up a history and personality for the newly-attired one.

" You are Mr. Isaacson," said he. " Here's the card of a Mr. Isaacson who called some time ago ; put it in your pocket. I will write you a couple of fake letters to back the card : you are in the watch trade. Pebblemarsh is the nearest town, only five miles down the road ; there's a station there, but you'd better avoid that. There's a garage. You could get a car to London. If they nail you, scream like an excited Jew, produce your credentials, and if the worst comes to the worst refer to me and come back here. I would love that interview. Country policemen, lunatic asylum man, Mr. Isaacson, highly excited, and myself."

He sat down to write the fake letters addressed to Mr. Isaacson by his uncle, Julius Goldberg, and his partner, Marcus Cohen. As he wrote he talked over his shoulder on the subject of disguises, alleging that the only really impenetrable disguise was that of a nigger minstrel.

" You see, all black faces are pretty much the same," said he. " Their predominant expression is black, but I haven't got the fixings nor the coloured pants and things, to say nothing of a banjo, so I reckon you'll just have to be Mr. Isaacson, and you may thank the God of the Hebrews I haven't made you an old clothes man—watches are respectable. Here are your letters, they are short but credible. Have you enough money ? "

" Lots," said Jones, " and I don't know in the least how to thank you for what you have done. I'd have been had, sure, wearing that hat and coat—well, maybe we'll meet again."

They parted at the gate, the hunted one taking the white, dusty road in the direction of Pebblemarsh, Kellerman watching till a bend hid him from view.

Kellerman had in some mysterious way added a touch of the footlights to this business. This confounded Kellerman, who thought in terms of reels and situations, had managed to inspire Jones with the feeling that he was moving on the screen, and that any moment the hedgerows might give up an army of pursuers, to the delight of a hidden audience.

However, the hedgerows of the Pebblemarsh road gave up nothing but the odours of briar and woodbine ; nothing pursued him but the twitter of birds and the songs of larks above the summer-drowsy fields.

There is nothing much better to live in the memory

than a real old English country road on a perfect summer afternoon, no pleasanter companion.

Pebblemarsh is a town of some four thousand souls. It possesses a dye factory. It once possessed the only really good trout stream in this part of the country, with the inevitable result, for in England when a really good trout stream is discovered a dye factory is always erected upon its banks. Pebblemarsh now only possesses a dye factory.

The main street runs north and south, and as Jones passed up it he might have fancied himself in Sandbourne or Northbourne, so much alike are these three towns.

Half-way up, and opposite the post office, an archway disclosed itself, with above it the magic word :

" GARAGE."

He entered the place. There were no signs of cars, nothing of a movable description in that yard, with the exception of a stout man in leggings and shirt-sleeves, who, seeing the stranger, came forward to receive him.

" Have you a car ? " asked Jones.

" They're all out except a Ford," said the stout man. " Did you want to go for a drive ? "

" No ; I want to run up to London in a hurry. What's the mileage from here ? "

" We reckon it sixty-three miles from here to London. That is to say, the Old Kent Road."

" That's near enough," said Jones. " What's the price ? "

" A shilling a mile to take you, and a sixpence a mile for the car coming back."

' What's the total ? "

The proprietor figured in his head for a moment.
" Four, fourteen, six," said he.

" I'll take the car," said Jones, " and I'll pay you
now.   Can I have it at once ? "

The proprietor went to a door and opened it.

" Jim," cried he, " are you there ?   Gentleman
wants the Ford taken to London.   Get her out and get
yourself ready."

He turned to Jones.

" She'll be ready in ten minutes, if that will do."

" That will do," said Jones, " and here's the money."

He waited whilst the Ford was taken from its den ;
then Jim, an inconspicuous looking man, wriggled
into his overcoat, the engine was started, and Jones
taking his seat, they were off.

They turned up the street and along the London
Road.   They passed a respectable cemetery, the dye
works, a tin chapel ; and the car taking a hill as Fords
know how, dropped Pebblemarsh to invisibility and
surrounded itself with vast stretches of green and sun-
warmed country.   Towards dusk they passed through
a large town, then another, and then came the lights
of London and an endless road, half road, half street.

Jim turned in his seat.   " This here is the Old Kent
Road," said he ; " which part did you want ? "

" This will do," said Jones.   " Pull her up."

He got out, took the four and sixpence from his
pocket and gave Jim two shillings for a tip.   Then
with only two and sixpence in the world, within touch,
he watched the car drive away before turning London-
wards.

The Old Kent Road was once, no doubt, a pleasant
enough place, but pleasure has long forsaken it, and
cleanliness.

It was here that David Copperfield sold his jacket,

and the old clothiers' shops are so antiquated that any
of them might have been the scene of the purchase.
To-night the Old Kent Road was swarming, and the
further Jones advanced towards the river the thicker
seemed the throng.

At a flaring public-house, and for the price of a
shilling, he obtained enough food in the way of sausages
and mashed potatoes to satisfy his hunger. A half-
pint tankard of beer completed the satisfaction of
the inner man, and, having bought a packet of navy
cut cigarettes and a box of matches, he left the place
and pursued his way towards the river.

He had exactly tenpence in his pocket, and he fell
to thinking as he walked of the extraordinary monetary
fluctuations he had experienced in this city of London.
At the "Savoy" that fatal day he had less than
ten pounds; next morning, though robed as a lord,
he had only a penny. The penny had been reduced
to a halfpenny by the purchase of a newspaper, the
halfpenny swollen to five pounds by Rochester's gift.
The five pounds sprang in five minutes to eight thousand, owing to Voles; the eight thousand to a million
eight thousand, owing to Mulhausen; Simms and
Cavendish had stripped him of his last cent; the
Smithers affair had given him nine pounds; now he
had only tenpence; and to-morrow, at nine o'clock,
he would have eight thousand !

It will be noted that he did not consider that eight
thousand his till it was safe in his pocket in the form of
notes; he had learned by bitter experience to put his
trust in nothing but the tangible. He reached the
river, and the great bridge that spans it here, and on
the bridge he paused, leaning his elbow on the parapet
and looking down stream.

The waning moon had risen, painting the water with

silver. Barge lights and the lights of tugs and police-boats showed points of orange and dribbles of ruffled gold, whilst away down stream, to the right, the airy, fairy tracery of the Houses of Parliament fretted the sky.

It was a nocturne after the heart of Whistler, and Jones, as he gazed at it, felt for the first time the magic of this wonderful, half-revealed city, with its million yellow eyes. He passed on, crossing to the right bank, and found the Strand. Here, in a bar, and for the price of half a pint of beer, he sat for some twenty minutes, watching the customers and killing time ; then, with his worldly wealth reduced to eight-pence, he wandered off westward, passing the " Savoy," and pausing for a moment to peep down the great archway at the gaily lit hotel.

At midnight he had gravitated to the Embankment, and found a seat not overcrowded.

Here he fell in with a gentleman, derelict like him-self—a free-spoken individual, whose conversation whiled away an hour.

CHAPTER XVI

THE BLIGHTED CITY

SAID the person, after a request for a match :
" Warm night, but there's a change in the
weather coming on, or I'm greatly mistaken. I've
lost nearly everything in the chops and changes of life,
but there's one thing I haven't lost—my barometer—
that's to say, my rheumatism. It tells me when rain
is coming as sure as an aneroid. London is pretty full
for the time of year, don't you think ? "

" Yes," said Jones ; " I reckon it is."

They talked, the gentleman with the barometer
passing from the weather to politics, from politics to
high finance, from high finance to himself. He had
been a solicitor.

" Disbarred, as you see, for nothing but what a
hundred men are doing at the present moment.
There's no justice in the world, except, maybe, in the
Law Courts. I'm not one of those who think the Law
is an ass ; no, there's a great deal of common sense
in the law of England. I'm not talking of the Incor-
porated Law Society, that shut me out from a living
for a slip any man might make, I'm talking of the old
laws of England as administered by his Majesty's
judges ; study them, and you will be astonished at
their straight common sense and justice. I'm not

holding a brief for lawyers—I'm frank, you see ; the
business of lawyers is to wriggle round and circumvent
the truth, to muddy evidence, confuse witnesses, and
undo justice—I'm just talking of the laws."

" Do you know anything of the laws of lunacy ? "
asked Jones.

" Something."

" I had a friend who was supposed to be suffering
from mind trouble ; two doctors doped him and put
him away in an asylum—he was quite harmless."

" What do you mean by doped him ? " asked the
other.

" Gave him a drug to quiet him, and then took
him off in an automobile."

" Was there money involved ? "

" You may say there was. He was worth a
million."

" Anyone to benefit by his being put away ? "

" Well, I expect one might make out a case of that
—the family would have the handling of the million,
wouldn't they ? "

" It all depends ; but there's one thing certain,
there'd be a thundering law case for any clever solicitor
to handle if the plaintiff were not too far gone in his
mind to plead.   Anyhow, the drugging is out of order
—whole thing sounds fishy."

" Suppose he escaped," said Jones.   " Could they
take him back by force ? "

" That's a difficult question to answer. If he were
cutting up shines it would be easy, but if he were
clever enough to pretend to be sane it might be
difficult.   You see, he would have to be arrested ; no
man can go up and seize another man in the street
and say, ' You're mad ; come along with me,' simply
because, even if he holds a certificate of lunacy against

the other man, the other man might say, ' You've made a mistake ; I'm not the person you want.' Then it would be a question of swearing before a magistrate. The good old laws of England are very strict about the freedom of the body and the rights of the individual man to be heard in his own defence. If your lunatic were not too insane, and were to take refuge in a friend's house, and the friend were to back him, that would make things more difficult still."

" If he were to take refuge in his own house ? "

" Oh, that would make the thing still more difficult, very much more so. If, of course, he were not conducting himself in a manner detrimental to the public peace, firing guns out of windows, and so forth. The laws of England are very strict about entering a man's house. Of course, were the pursuers to go before a magistrate and swear that the pursued were a dangerous lunatic, then a right of search and entry might be obtained, but on the pursuers would lie the onus of proof. Now, pauper lunatics are very easily dealt with ; the relieving officer, on the strength of a certificate of lunacy, can go to the poor man's cottage or tenement and take him away, for, you see, the man possessing no property, it is supposed that no man is interested in his internment, but once introduce the property element and there is the very devil to pay, especially in cases where the lunatic is only eccentric, and does not come into court with straws in his hair, so to speak."

" I get you," said Jones.

He offered cigarettes, and presently the communicative one departed, having borrowed fourpence on the strength of his professional advice.

The rest of that night was a very good imitation of a nightmare. Jones tried several different seats in succession, and managed to do a good deal of walking. Dawn found him on London Bridge, watching the birth of another perfect day, but without enthusiasm.

He was cheerful, but tired. The thought that, at nine o'clock or thereabouts, he would be able to place his hand on eight thousand pounds, gave him the material for his cheerfulness. He had often read of the joy of open-air life, and the freedom of the hobo, but open-air life in London, on looking back upon it, did not appeal to him. He had been twice moved on by policemen, and his next-door neighbours, after the departure of the barometer man, were of a type that inspired neither liking nor trust.

He heard Big Ben booming six o'clock. He had three hours still before him, and he determined to take it out in walking. He would go citywards, and then come back with an appetite for breakfast.

Having made this resolve, he started, passing through the deserted streets till he reached the Bank, and then onwards till he reached the Mile End Road.

As he walked on he made plans. When he had drawn his money he would breakfast at a restaurant; he fixed upon Romano's—eggs and bacon and sausages, coffee and hot rolls would be the menu. Then he fell to wondering whether Romano's would be open for breakfasts, or whether it was of the type that only serves luncheons and dinners. If it were, then he could breakfast at the Charing Cross Hotel.

These considerations led him a good distance on his way. Then the Mile End Road beguiled him, lying straight and foreign looking and empty in the sunlight. The barometer man's weather apparatus must have been at fault, for in all the sky there was not a cloud, nor the symptom of the coming of a cloud.

Away down near the docks, a clock over a public-house pointed to half-past seven, and he judged it time to return.

He came back. The Mile End Road was still deserted, the City round the Bank was destitute of life, Fleet Street empty.

Pompeii lay not more utterly dead than this weird city of vast business palaces, and the Strand showed nothing of life, or almost nothing, every shop was shuttered, though now it was close upon nine o'clock.

Something had happened to London, some blight had fallen on the inhabitants, death seemed everywhere, not seen but hinted at. Stray recollections of weird stories by H. G. Wells passed through the mind of Jones. He recalled the City of London when the Martians had done with it, that city of death and horror and sunlight and silence.

Then, of a sudden, as he neared the Law Courts, the appalling truth suddenly suggested itself to him.

He walked up to a policeman on point duty at a corner, a policeman who seemed under the mesmerism of the general gloom and blight, a policeman who might have been the blue concrete core of negation.

" Say, officer," said Jones, " what day's to-day ? "

" Sunday," said the policeman.

CHAPTER XVII

A JUST MAN ANGERED

WHEN things are piled one on top of another beyond a certain height they generally come down with a crash.

That one word " Sunday " was the last straw for Jones, sweeping away breakfast, bank, and everything—coming on top of the events of the last twenty-four hours it brought his mental complacency to ruins, ruins from which shot blazing jets of wrath.

Red rage filled him. He had been made game of, every man and everything was against him. Well, he would bite. He would strike. He would attack, careless of everything, heedless of everything.

A mesmerised-looking taxicab, crawling along on the opposite side of the way, fortunately caught his eye.

" I'll make hay ! " cried Jones, as he rushed across the street.

He stopped the cab.

" 10A, Carlton House Terrace," he cried to the driver.

He got in and shut the door with a bang.

He got out at Carlton House Terrace, ran up the steps of 10A, and rang the bell.

The door was opened by the man who had helped to eject Spicer. He did not seem in the least surprised to see Jones.

" Pay that taxi," said Jones.

" Yes, my lord," replied the flunkey.

Jones, all through his adventures since leaving Hoover's, had never bothered about his extraordinary get up. His present attire did not seem to him especially incongruous, nor did it to that wonderful servant who took the cap handed to him as carefully as though it had been a guinea Lincoln Bennett, whilst Jones turned to the breakfast-room.

The faint smell of coffee met him at the door as he opened it. There were no servants in the room. Only a woman, quietly breakfasting, with the " Life of St. Thomas à Kempis " by her plate.

It was Venetia Birdbrook.

She half rose from her chair when she saw Jones. He shut the door. The sight of Venetia acted upon him almost as badly as the word " Sunday " had done.

" What are you doing here ? " said he. " I know—you and that lot had me tucked away in a lunatic asylum ; now you have taken possession of the house."

Venetia was quite calm.

" Since the house is not yours," said she, " I fail to see how my presence here affects you. We know the truth. Dr. Simms has arrived at the conclusion that your confession was at least based on truth. That you are what you proclaimed yourself to be, a man named Jones. We thought you were mad ; we see now that you are an impostor. Kindly leave this house, or I will call for a policeman."

Jones's mind lost all its fire. Hatred can cool as well as inflame, and he hated Venetia and all her belongings, including her dowager mother and her uncle the duke, with a hatred well based on reason and fact.

" I don't know what you are talking about," said

he. " Do you mean that joke I played on you all ?
I am the Earl of Rochester, this is my house, and I
request you to leave it. Don't speak ! I know what
you are going to say. You and your family will do
this, and you will do that. You will do nothing.
Even if I were an impostor, you would dare to do
nothing. Your family washing is far, far too much
soiled to expose it in public.

" If I were an impostor, who can say I have not
played an honourable game ? I have recovered
valuable property—did I touch it and take it away ?
Did I expose to the public an affair that would have
caused a scandal ? You will do nothing, and you
know it. You did not even dare to tell the servants
here what has happened, for the servant who let me
in was not a bit surprised. Now, if you have finished
your breakfast, will you kindly leave my house."

Venetia rose and took up her book.

" *Your* house ! " said she.

" Yes, my house. From this day forth, my house.
But that is not all. To-morrow I will get lawyers to
work, and I'll get apologies as big as houses from the
whole lot of you, else I'll prosecute." He was getting
angry. " Prosecute you for doping me." Recollections of the barometer man's advice came to him.
" Doping me in order to lay your hands on that million
of money."

He went to the bell and rang it.

" We want no scene before the servants," said
Venetia hurriedly.

" Then kindly go," said Jones, " or you will have
a perfect panorama before the servants."

She left the room.

A servant entered.

" Send Church here," said Jones.

He was trembling like a furious dog.

He had got the whole situation in hand. He had told his tale and acted like an honourable man ; the fools had disbelieved him and doped him. They had scented the truth, but they dared do nothing. Mulhausen and the recovered mine, the Plinlimon letters, Rochester's past, all these were his bastions, to say nothing of Rochester's suicide.

The fear of publicity held them in a vice. Even were they to go to America, and prove that a man called Jones, exactly like the Earl of Rochester, had lived in Philadelphia, go to the " Savoy " and prove that a man exactly like the Earl of Rochester had lived there, produce the clothes he had come home in that night—all of that would lead them where—to an action at law.

They could not arrest him as an impostor till they had proved him an impostor. To prove that, they would have to turn the family history inside out before a gaping public.

Mr. Church came in.

" Church," said Jones, " I played a practical joke on—on my people. I met a certain man called Jones at the ' Savoy.' Well, we needn't go into details ; he was very like me, and I told my people for a joke that I was Jones. The fools thought I was mad. They called in two doctors, and drugged me and hauled me off to a place. I got out, and here I am back. What do you think of that ? "

" Well, my lord," said Church, " if I may say it to you, those practical jokes are dangerous things to play. Lord Llangwathby——"

" Was he here ? "

" He came last night, my lord, to have a personal explanation about a telegram he said you sent him as a practical joke some time ago, taking him up to Cumberland."

" I'll never play another," said Jones. " Tell them to bring me some breakfast. And look here, Church, I've told my sister to leave the house at once. I want no more of her here. See that her luggage is taken down at once."

" Yes, my lord."

" And see here, Church, let no one in. Lord Llangwathby or anyone else. I want a little peace. By the way, have a taxi sent for, and tell me when my sister's luggage is down."

In the middle of breakfast Church came in to say that Lady Venetia was departing, and Jones came into the hall to verify the fact.

Venetia had brought a crocodile-skin travelling-bag and a trunk.

These were being conveyed to a taxi.

Not one word did she say to relieve her outraged feelings. The fear of a " scene before the servants " kept her quiet.

CHAPTER XVIII

HE FINDS HIMSELF

THAT evening at nine o'clock Jones sat in the smoking-room, writing. He had trusted Church with an important mission, on the upshot of which his future depended.

If you will review his story, as he himself was reviewing it now, you will see that, despite a strong will and a mind quick to act, the freedom of his will had always been hampered by circumstance.

Circumstance from the first had determined that he should be a lord.

I leave it to philosophers to determine what circumstance is. I can only say that, from a fair knowledge of life, circumstance seems to me more than a fortuitous happening of things. Who does not know the man of integrity and ability, the man destined for the presidency or the college chair, who remains in an office all his life. Luck is somehow against him, or the man who starts in life with everything against him who arrives, not by creeping, but by leaps and bounds.

I do not wish to cast a shade on individual effort, I only say this. If you ever find circumstance, whose other name is fortune, feeling for you in order to make you a lord, don't kick; for when fortune takes an interest in a man she is cunning as a woman. She is a woman, in fact.

At half-past nine a knock came to the door. It was opened by Church, who ushered in Teresa, Countess of Rochester.

Jones rose from his chair, Church shut the door, and they found themselves face to face.

The girl did not sit down, she stood holding the back of a chair, and looking at the man before her. She looked scared, dazed, like a person suddenly awakened from sleep in a strange place.

Jones knew at once.

" You have guessed the truth," said he, " that I am not your husband ? "

" I knew it," she replied, " when you told us in the drawing-room. The others thought you mad. I knew you were speaking the truth."

" That was why you ran from the room ? "

" Yes. What more have you to say ? "

" I have a very great deal more to say. Will you not sit down ? "

She sat down on the edge of a chair, folded her hands, and continued looking at him with that scared, hunted expression.

" I want to say just this," said Jones. " Right through this business, I have tried to play a straight game. I can guess from your face that you fear me as if I were something horrible. I don't blame you. I ask you to listen to me.

" Your husband took advantage of two facts—the fact that I am his twin image, as he called it, and the fact that I was temporarily without money and stranded in London. I am not a drunkard, but that night I came under the influence of drink. He took advantage of that to send me home as himself. I am going to say a nasty thing. That was not the action of a gentleman."

The girl winced.

"Never," went on Jones, "would I say things against a man who is dead, yet I am forced to tell you the truth, so that you may see this man as he was. Wait."

He went to the bureau and took out some papers. He handed her one.   She read :

"Stick to it, if you can, I could not.—ROCHESTER."

"That is your husband's handwriting ? "

"Yes."

"Now, think for a moment of his act as regards yourself. He sent me, a stranger, home, never thinking a thought about you."

Her breath choked back.

"As for me," went on Jones, "from the first moment I saw you I have thought of your welfare. I told my story for your sake, so that things might be cleared up, and they put me in an asylum for my pains. I escaped ; and for your sake I am saying all this. Does it give me pleasure to show you your husband's character ? I would sooner cut off my right hand, but that would not help you. You have got to know, else I cannot possibly get out of this. Read these."

He handed her the Plinlimon letters.

She read them carefully. Whilst she was doing so he sat down and waited.

"These were written two years ago," said she in a sad voice, as she folded them together, "a year after we were married."

It was the tone of the voice that did it ; as she

handed the letters back to him she saw that his eyes were filled with tears.

He put them back in the bureau without a word. He felt that he had struck the innocent again and most cruelly.

Then he came back to the chair on which he had been sitting, and stood holding its back.

" You see how we are both placed ? " said he. " To prove your husband's death, all my business would have to be raked up. I don't mind, because I have acted straight ; but you would mind. The fact of his suicide, the fact of his sending me home—everything that would hit you again and again. Yet look at your position—I do not know what we are to do. If I go away and go back to the States, I leave you before the world as the wife of a man still living who has deserted you ; if I stay and go on being the Earl of Rochester, you are tied to a phantom."

He paced the floor, head down, wrestling with an insoluble problem, whilst she sat looking at him.

" Which is the easiest for you ? " asked she.

" Oh, me ! " said he ; " I'm not thinking of myself—back to the States, of course ; but that's out of the question. There are lots of easy things to do, but when my case comes in contact with yours there's nothing easy to do. Do you think it was easy for me to go off that night and leave you waiting for me, feeling that you thought me a skunk ? No, that was not easy."

She had been sitting very calm and still up till now ; then suddenly she looked down. She burst into tears.

" Oh," she cried, " why were you not him ? If he had only been you ! He cared nothing for me ; yet I loved him—you—you——"

"I care for nothing at all but you," said he.

She shuddered and turned her head away.

"That's the mischief of it, as far as I am concerned," he went on. "I can't escape without injuring you, and so myself; yet I don't wonder at your hating me."

She turned her face to him, it was flushed and wet.

"I do not hate you," said she; "you are the only man I ever met—unselfish!"

"No," he said, "I'm selfish. It's just because I love you that I think of you more than myself, and I love you because you are good and sweet. If you were another woman, I would not bother about you. I'd be cruel enough, I reckon, and go off and leave you tied up, and get back to the States; but you are you, and that's my bother. I did not know till now how I was tied to you; yesterday at that asylum place, and all last night, I did not think of you. I came here to-day driven by want of money. I was so angry with the whole business, I determined to go on being Rochester; then you came into my mind, and I sent Church to ask you to come and see me— much good it has done!"

"I don't know," she said.

He looked at her quickly. Her glance fell.

Next moment he was beside her, kneeling and holding her hand.

For a moment they said not one word. Then he spoke as though answering questions.

"We can get married—oh, I don't mind going on being the Earl of Rochester. There were times when I thought I'd go cracked, but now you know the truth I reckon I can go on pretending. People can have the marriage ceremony performed twice—of course, it would have to be private—I don't believe you can ever care for me—I don't know, maybe you will. Do you care for me for myself in the least ? I reckon I'm half mad ; but, say, when did you begin to like me for myself—was it only just because you thought I was unselfish—was it ? "

" If I like you at all," she said, with a little catch in her voice. " Perhaps it was that—night——"

" What night ? "

" The night you struck——"

" The Russian ; but you thought I was *him* then."

" Perhaps," said she dreamily ; " but I thought it was unlike him—do you understand ? "

" I don't know. I understand nothing but that I have got you to care for always—to worship."

*   *   *   *   *   *

" Good-night," said she at last.

She was standing, preparing to go.

" The family know the truth—at least, they are sure of the truth ; but, as you say, they can do nothing. Imagine their feelings when I tell them what we have agreed on ! With me on your side, they are absolutely helpless."

*   *   *   *   *   *

There is, fortunately enough, no law preventing two married people being re-married privately, the good old lawyers of England considering, no doubt, that a man having gone through the ceremony once would think it enough.

They were married a week later.

*   *   *   *   *   *

All this happened some years ago—years marked by some very practical and brilliant speeches in the House of Lords. It is a queer story, but not queerer than the face of the Dowager Countess of Rochester when she reads in private all the nice complimentary things that the papers have to say about her son.

THE END

Printed at The Chapel River Press, Kingston, Surrey.

Trieste

Trieste Publishing has a massive catalogue of classic book titles. Our aim is to provide readers with the highest quality reproductions of fiction and non-fiction literature that has stood the test of time. The many thousands of books in our collection have been sourced from libraries and private collections around the world.

The titles that Trieste Publishing has chosen to be part of the collection have been scanned to simulate the original. Our readers see the books the same way that their first readers did decades or a hundred or more years ago. Books from that period are often spoiled by imperfections that did not exist in the original. Imperfections could be in the form of blurred text, photographs, or missing pages. It is highly unlikely that this would occur with one of our books. Our extensive quality control ensures that the readers of Trieste Publishing's books will be delighted with their purchase. Our staff has thoroughly reviewed every page of all the books in the collection, repairing, or if necessary, rejecting titles that are not of the highest quality. This process ensures that the reader of one of Trieste Publishing's titles receives a volume that faithfully reproduces the original, and to the maximum degree possible, gives them the experience of owning the original work.

We pride ourselves on not only creating a pathway to an extensive reservoir of books of the finest quality, but also providing value to every one of our readers. Generally, Trieste books are purchased singly - on demand, however they may also be purchased in bulk. Readers interested in bulk purchases are invited to contact us directly to enquire about our tailored bulk rates. Email: customerservice@triestepublishing.com

You May Also Like

ISBN: 9781760579685
Paperback: 156 pages
Dimensions: 6.14 x 0.33 x 9.21 inches
Language: eng

A Summary of the Principal Evidences for the Truth & Divine Origin of the Christian Revelation. To Which Is Added the Celebrated Poem on Death. Designed Chiefly for the Use of Young Persons

Beilby Porteus

ISBN: 9781760571467
Paperback: 242 pages
Dimensions: 6.14 x 0.51 x 9.21 inches
Language: eng

Reminiscences of an Indianian: From the Sassafras Log behind the Barn in Posey County to Broader Fields

J. A. Lemcke

You May Also Like

ISBN: 9780649271740
Paperback: 56 pages
Dimensions: 6.0 x 0.12 x 9.0 inches
Language: eng

Chenar Leaves: Poems of Kashmir

Mrs. Percy Brown

ISBN: 9781760579623
Paperback: 138 pages
Dimensions: 6.14 x 0.30 x 9.21 inches
Language: eng

Life Long Musings; Or, Fragments Gathered by the Way; A Collection of Poems

David E. Dodge

You May Also Like

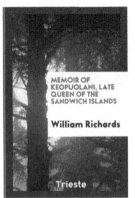

Memoir of Keopuolani, Late Queen of the Sandwich Islands

William Richards

ISBN: 9781760570453
Paperback: 68 pages
Dimensions: 6.14 x 0.14 x 9.21 inches
Language: eng

Fugitive Poetry

N. P. Willis

ISBN: 9781760579159
Paperback: 104 pages
Dimensions: 6.14 x 0.22 x 9.21 inches
Language: eng

www.triestepublishing.com

You May Also Like

Elektra

Sophocles

ISBN: 9780649019144
Paperback: 80 pages
Dimensions: 6.14 x 0.17 x 9.21 inches
Language: eng

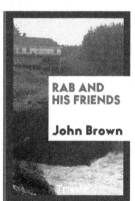

Rab and His Friends

John Brown

ISBN: 9780649019175
Paperback: 78 pages
Dimensions: 6.14 x 0.16 x 9.21 inches
Language: eng

Find more of our titles on our website. We have a selection of thousands of titles that will interest you. Please visit

www.triestepublishing.com

Lightning Source UK Ltd.
Milton Keynes UK
UKOW01f2109060917
308727UK00005B/311/P